MIND GAMES

GORDON POPE THRILLERS, BOOK 2

B. B. GRIFFITH

Griffith Publishing
Denver

Publication Information

Mind Games

ISBN: 978-0-9963726-7-1

Written by B. B. Griffith

Cover design by James T. Egan of Bookfly Design

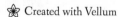 Created with Vellum

To Jay, who is always an inspiration.

"Sometimes I think people take reality for granted."

—Alex Ridgemont
Made You Up by Francesca Zappia

CHAPTER ONE

Sophie's walk home from school was starting to scare her.

Most of the kids at Merryville Preparatory Academy didn't walk home from school. Most kids she went to school with had parents or chauffeurs pick them up, but Sophie's mom was very busy writing her book in the afternoons and often forgot about her. So Sophie walked.

Most of the time, Sophie's walks were uneventful. She knew five blocks shouldn't be a problem for a girl to walk. Especially a girl just turned twelve. She'd be a teenager soon. Teenagers were supposed to do things like walk here and there alone and not be scared. Especially in Merryville. Sophie knew bad things sometimes happened to girls who walked alone in Baltimore, but not in Merryville. Merryville had gates. Merryville had guards. The families that lived in Merryville paid a lot of money to stay safe and quiet and keep those bad things outside.

Sophie told herself all of those things over and over again. But something still followed her. What stalked

Sophie seemed to walk through gates and couldn't care less about guards. What stalked Sophie was already on the inside.

How he'd gotten on the inside, she couldn't say. He was the exact type of person that the gates were built for, that the guards were paid to guard against. His name was Mo, and Sophie knew him well. She always knew when he was nearby. She got a prickly feeling of anticipation—like when the towering trees above her rustled with a cold autumn wind she couldn't feel yet but knew would hit her soon. That was Mo. A distant murmuring that made her stomach twinge. A soft muttering that grew stronger with every step she took until Sophie could practically hear his words, which were always the same.

All Mo talked about was fire.

Sophie's house was at the end of a softly curving street called Long Lane, where the addresses all had single digits. The street was wide but empty, the sidewalks pristine and white, as if the leaves themselves avoided them in their fall-ing. As she walked, she kept hoping for a car to come or a dog to bark or a door to slam—anything to make her feel like just a normal girl walking home from school in a normal neighborhood, back to her normal home and normal mom. But no cars came, and no dogs barked. Merryville was as quiet as always, except for the murmuring trees and the scattered-sand sound of the leaves bumping down the street behind her.

The autumn wind she'd heard in the distance finally caught up, gusting her long blond hair forward and twisting it about her face as she was swirled in a tornado of fallen leaves the color of flame. She brushed them from her hair and plucked them from her plaid dress uniform as she walked. She wiped her hands instinctively on her bony hips. Leaves were dirty. They'd been lying on the street, and the cars rolled on the street, and the tires on the cars had been all over—even into the parts of Baltimore where bad things happened to girls who walked alone—and they brought their dirt from the bad parts past the gates and into Merryville. Onto the leaves. And then into her hair.

Sophie felt her heart racing. She focused on stepping over the cracks on the sidewalk. She focused on taking the same number of steps between each crack. She focused on counting.

A shadow flitted across the street. Sophie forced herself not to follow it with her eyes. She tucked her thumbs more tightly around the straps of her backpack and kept counting and kept walking—faster but not too fast. Too fast, and Mo would notice her.

She told herself the shadow she'd seen was a tendril of cloud skittering in front of the weak autumn sun. It had to be. It just had to be because her mom had told her time and time again that Mo wasn't real. Mo was imaginary. Mo was an imaginary friend that had lived in Sophie's mind for years.

And maybe that was true, once. Back when Mo had tea parties with her. Back when Mo played the guy dolls so Sophie could play the girl dolls. Back when Mo would help her hide in piles of stuffed animals when her mom and dad screamed at each other. Back when she was a little kid that cared about tea parties and dolls and stuffed animals and was scared at how quiet the house was after her dad moved away. But then she became twelve, which is almost thirteen. She was used to being alone now. She was used to having a mom that was busy writing her book. That's when imaginary friends are supposed to disappear. The funny thing was, in a lot of ways, Mo *had* stopped being imaginary. The not-so-funny thing was Mo didn't feel imaginary anymore because he felt more real every day.

Another flitting shadow, and not a cloud in the sky. The breeze was heavier in the canopies. The leaves clattered against the looming red-brick façades of the houses she passed, and they stuck like swarming bees in the hedges that separated the estates. Her plaid dress strained at the boxy outline of her coltish frame. For a moment, all she heard was the roar of the leaves, and all she saw was the blond explosion of her own hair, but then she heard something else.

You're all alone, Sophie.

A soft press on her back, between her shoulder blades.

She whipped around, the wind blowing her eyes clear once more. Nobody there. But Sophie knew better.

The tricky thing about Mo was that he was fast. She rarely saw him, but she could hear him. When he decided to speak up, she could hear him anywhere. Mo was especially fond of sewers. That was why Sophie sprinted over every storm drain and eyed every manhole with her knuckles white around the straps of her backpack.

A gleaming black sedan came around the bend. Sophie recognized it as belonging to one of the chauffeurs from school, and she thought about crying out and asking for a ride, just for the next three blocks. But she couldn't risk the driver talking to her mom and her mom asking why Sophie seemed incapable of walking five blocks from school.

Her mom, Dianne West, could never know that Mo might be creeping around again. That, as she liked to say, "just wouldn't do. Not for a girl your age, Sophia Alexandra West. Not any longer."

Sophie thought she saw the brim of a baseball cap dart back down behind the iron gate of her neighbors' drive. She froze in between cracks on the sidewalk, then against her better judgment, she craned her neck for another look. The gate was swathed with ivy in an explosion of fall colors, and she couldn't make out anything on the other side, but something rustled. She backed away, not realizing how close she'd come to the storm drain until it was too late.

Nowhere is safe, Sophie.

Sophie managed to clip her scream off at a yelp then took off at an awkward lope along the far edge of the sidewalk. Her heart raced, and the sound of it hammering in her chest mixed with the rattles of the leaves, and in that instant, she heard Mo all around her.

Burn it.

Burn it, Sophie.

Burn it all down.

His words hissed with the wind, rolled together in one long whisper.

"You're not real," Sophie said, gritting her teeth through tears that were blown dry as soon as they trickled down her face. "Mom says you're not real."

But even as she spoke, she could feel Mo beneath her, dashing along through the pipes. She could picture him: the laces of his sneakers untied and flopping and the cuffs of his blue jeans trailing in the muck. His white T-shirt would be grubby, as always, and his black baseball cap, a size too big, plunked down low so the brim shaded his eyes and all she'd see was a full set of grinning teeth. He was straining toward her from below, running along the far right side of the pipe so as to be right under her, step for step. She just knew it. Even though her mom said it couldn't be.

Sophie saw another storm drain ahead and stopped. Only a block until home—but it might as well have been a mile. Mo was getting louder—louder than he'd been in a long time, in years and years. Only one other time could she remember Mo having been so loud. That time, he'd gotten her in a lot of trouble. That was how she lost her tree house to the flames. And the big backyard tree to the flames. And almost the entire west wing of the house to the flames.

The wind died down, and Mo's voice went with it, but Sophie knew better. She stared at the dark slot of drain, her shoulder muscles shaking, her scuffed white hush puppies pigeon-toed under knees that felt like giving out. The longer she stared at the black of that place, the more she saw. First, a little wiggle of movement in the dark. Then the black swirled into different shapes. A body? A ball cap?

Sophie shook her head violently. Kids don't hang out in sewers. Not real kids, not imaginary kids. Nobody hangs out in sewers. It was impossible. All of it was impossible. She set herself, pushing her back straight, the way her mom had always told her. She held her chin high. She swallowed hard and started forward. The gutter loomed. She wanted nothing but to run to the middle of the street, but that would be the final straw. That would be admitting he was back. Her skinny ankles passed within a foot of the drain. Her arms puckered with gooseflesh, but she forced herself to walk at a normal pace. One step. Another. She sagged with relief. She was imagining things after all. Mo was gone. She turned away from the grate. She'd been staring at the dark slot with such force she felt her neck crackle with tension. She could finally swallow. She saw the gate in front of her own drive. It was already open, beckoning her home. He was all in her mind, just like her mom said.

In her haste to get home, she stepped on a crack. She

could feel it soil her like gum on the bottom of her shoes, and she shuddered. She wiped her shoes on the lawn nearby, stepped back to just past the previous crack, then counted off again… and when she looked up at her house, Mo was standing in her driveway.

He stood like a skinny superhero with a gaunt grin. Hands on hips. Chest puffed out. His mouth never moved from that smile, but over the years, Sophie had learned to recognize his mood from the expressions of his eyes. Back when Mo was her friend and didn't scare her so much, his eyes had laughed. Not anymore. Now his eyes were screaming.

His voice rang loud and clear in her head. *The only way to stay safe is to burn it all.*

Sophie grabbed her head in her hands, wrenching it back and forth, and the wind roared down the wide street of her block, raking empty sidewalks, buffeting against closed gates, and screaming past enormous locked doors. She ran toward him, toward her bedroom in the house behind him, where she would be safe. She expected to run right into him, but she never did. She managed to look up, blinking through tears, at the point at which she thought she'd hit him, but she found nothing. No sign of him. No sign of anyone. Nothing but the wind.

Long after she slammed the front door behind her, long after she shed her backpack in the anteroom, long after she ran up the first flight of stairs and threw herself, moaning, onto her bed, the wind still carried his voice.

Burn it, Sophie.

It's the only way to stay safe.

Burn it all.

The worst part, the part that struck at her with more raw fear than even that moment where her exposed ankle had been inches from the gaping darkness of the sewer, was that she knew he was right. In her heart of hearts, she knew Mo was right. She had to burn it. That was the only way to stay safe, to keep her mom safe, to keep everyone safe. Everything was so *dirty*. It all had to go.

For Sophie, it was burn or die.

CHAPTER TWO

Dianne West did not recognize the shrill scream of the fire alarm at first. She thought the sound might be some sort of ludicrous bird gone completely off its rocker on the balcony. She even looked out of the window of her study, left and right, and searched the trees for a few moments in a bit of a stupor. She got that way when writing her memoirs—hard to bring back. Her writing was like a deep dive, and she needed to come back in stages.

With another span of steady bleating from the hallway, she came to her senses. No bird sounded like that. She recognized the cacophony. She hadn't heard it for some time, but she had heard it before. She shot up out of her seat, shut the window so the neighbors wouldn't hear, saved her work, and started running. She ran out of her bedroom, her slippered feet slapping softly against the runner carpet in the great hallway of the second floor, all the way to the stairs, where she found the keypad. She'd marked where the keypad was affixed two years before, under similar circumstances. She knew those systems called the fire department outright after sixty seconds if you didn't key in an all-clear code. The fire brigade was the last thing she needed.

She flipped open the terminal, keyed in the code, and waited with bated breath for a half second until the alarm silenced. She sagged against the wall in momentary relief. Step one accomplished.

Now to find the fire.

Dianne followed her nose. She sniffed around the hallway overlooking the foyer then took a few steps down toward the landing between the ground floor and the second after tightening her robe around her. She smelled nothing downstairs. She turned around, stepped up, walking faster, her nose in the air. She didn't call Sophie's name. She knew that would have no effect at that point or might actually make things worse. She had to find her daughter herself.

Dianne walked past her bedroom chamber toward the library. There it was. There was the smell. The steely tang of struck matches, then below that smell, something sweeter. Almost like tobacco. Dianne stopped at Sophie's room. The door was closed. She threw it open. The air there was slightly hazy but with no sign of fire. No sign of Sophie, either, beyond her meticulously ordered art supplies and the rumpled spot on top of the comforter. Of course she wouldn't set fire to her own room. That was the only place she seemed not to mind going those days. But she was close.

Dianne set off down the hall again, testing doors at random, most locked. Some opened into the stuffy black-ness of curtains long drawn. Smoke that had merely blurred the edges of the room now stung her eyes then became a fog. Dianne knew what was burning. No more testing of doors. She quickly padded her way down the hall toward the library, and there she found the fire. It was a pile of old books set carefully in the center of the wooden floor. Beneath them, a pile of fallen leaves had burned to crinkled ash, which was already floating in the air. The books were fully engulfed, the flames half Dianne's height already. The fire was the second most substantial that Sophie had set... that Dianne knew about, anyway. Thankfully, it was still confined to twenty or so books in the middle of an otherwise empty room, one that, if Dianne were being frank, she hadn't entered in months. The wood would have to be refinished, of course. But the room—and the west wing—would air out. If she could put it out.

She eyed the curtains. She'd brought in the velvet from Cairo specifically for the library. Tough loss. She ran over to the nearest and yanked down hard. Dianne was a slight woman, shorter than her daughter since Sophie seemed to have shot up like a reed, and she'd neglected her personal trainer recently in favor of the memoir, but she still had wiry strength. After hanging on the velvet for a few moments, she heard a pop and saw a fastener shoot off into the haze. More pops, then a snap. The curtain fell over her. She threw it off herself, the first real notes of panic striking her, until she was free once more. Then she dragged it behind her like a royal train. She bunched the curtain in both fists and heaved it over the burning pile, then piled it on top of itself until it looked like a huge velvet beehive. The fire had grown by then, but it was no match for the heavy curtain. Dianne slapped at it with her slipper, crunching the burned books and ash and half-burned leaves underneath until it was spread out evenly under the curtains and the smoke creeping out from the sides guttered then quit.

Dianne peeked under the curtain. A waft of smoke caught her in the face, but it was dead smoke, dark as the ashes underneath. She let the curtain flop and nodded in admiration at the velvet. Looking at it from on high, one would never know it had burned at all. She'd get the exact same style. And clean the opposite curtain. And the upholstery. The smell just wouldn't do. Not even a hint of it. If there was even a hint, she'd throw everything out and redecorate.

Dianne opened the windows, wiped her brow, and turned around. Second objective accomplished. Next, to find her daughter.

Dianne checked in the gap behind the sofa against the far wall but found nothing. She eased onto her knees on the hardwood floor and looked low. Nothing. She shook her head and bit her upper lip. Sophie wouldn't be there, by the fire. When she was under one of her spells, she followed a certain pattern.

Dianne stepped out into the hall and straightened her back. She already felt better. If she could compartmentalize issues, setting them in little boxes in her mind, she could tackle them. The alarm settled was one compartment, set away. Next, the fire was set away. She would find Sophie too and set that away. Then she would get back to her memoir and eventually, when it was perfect, set that away too. The fire was a minor setback. That was all.

Dianne moved over to the wallpaper, a felted white fiber blend imported from Chamonix, raised at the fleur-de-lis patterning. She ran her fingers along it, her eyes peering until she found what she was looking for: a faint line of colored pencil, left as if an afterthought, like someone lazily trailing a finger in water.

That time, the color was orange. Dianne followed the thin trail as it bumped on and off and in between the raised fleurs-de-lis, out of the room, around the corner, and down the hall. Soon enough, she didn't need the trail any longer, for she could hear the whimpering—more than whimpering, actually. Something in the timbre of the sound reminded Dianne more of full-blown crying, only muffled, as though Sophie was sobbing, but into a pillow.

The end of the hallway rounded off into a circular sunroom ringed with windows that let in the final slanted rays of the hollow afternoon sun, all light and no heat at that time of the year. The windows had seated window wells with matching cushions, and in the leftmost window well, she found Sophie, crying into her dress. She'd pulled it up and over her head and stuffed a ball of the fabric into her mouth. She lay on her side, her skinny legs pulled up into her chest, her long, bony back exposed to Dianne. She was rocking slightly on her side. The orange pencil lay on the floor below the seat.

Dianne covered her mouth to stifle her disappointed cry. She'd seen Sophie in the midst of her episodes before, but never as bad as that. She'd been prepared to find her daughter wandering, maybe sitting dazed on the floor, legs crossed, back slumped, as she had been after the tree-house fire. But this... this looked as if she was in physical pain. This was a definite regression.

"Sophie? Sophie, honey. Can you hear me?"

Nothing. Muffled sobs. Steady rocking.

Dianne moved over to her daughter and gently put her hand on the small of her back. Rather than calming her, that seemed to shock Sophie. She spat out the fabric and wailed from underneath her dress.

"It's the only way! If I don't burn it, they'll come in! They'll take me! They'll murder me! They'll murder every-one! Mo told me! Mo told me! Mo told me!"

Dianne jerked her hand back as if burned. Sophie

grabbed a fistful of fabric from under her dress and jammed it into her mouth again, as if it was a leaking faucet she was helpless to stop.

So Mo was back. Dianne had been afraid that might happen. She'd suspected something along those lines ever since Sophie started talking to herself again. Not in public, of course, but here and there. Walking past Sophie's bedroom, Dianne would catch snippets of conversation. She kept the house silent when she wrote. Sounds traveled.

But what to do? Dianne absolutely would not brook a hospital. No emergency medical care of any sort. An ambulance rolling in through Merryville to pick up her raving daughter would be even worse than the fire brigade. At least with the fire brigade, she could come up with some other excuse, a faulty fuse or the cleaning people accidentally turning on a burner or something. Much harder to explain away an ambulance.

But Sophie needed help. The sounds she was making struck Dianne to the core. No daughter of hers should be in that much distress. She wouldn't stand for it. If only she knew of some way to mollify her, to reach her child in the depths of whatever hell she'd fallen into and pull her back. Clearly, Sophie was undergoing a mental break of some sort. What the girl needed more than anything, more than a hospital or an ambulance, was a psychiatrist.

Dianne narrowed her eyes in thought. Hadn't she read something about a child psychiatrist? Maybe she'd seen it on the news, briefly, as she watched television in bed, trying to rouse herself after one of her marathon writing sessions, perhaps a month before. The details were coming back to her. She could picture him in the awkward local-news interview. He was a sort of sad-looking fellow—handsome in a weary way, a little soft about the waist, with wire-frame glasses and more scruff on his chin than he had on the top of his head. He'd spoken all of ten seconds or so before they cut to some sports news, but he'd had a calm, steady voice, talking about... sleepwalking. That was it. Kids sleep-walking in East Baltimore. Dreadful. But he'd been up to the challenge. What was his name, again?

Dianne took a long look at her daughter, her eyes softening.

Pope. That was it. Gordon Pope. A compassionate last name. Maybe he could help. She reached into her dressing gown and pulled out her phone.

CHAPTER THREE

In the palm of his hand, Gordon Pope was spinning a large novelty pencil that read "World's Greatest Psychiatrist" while staring at his office clock, waiting for it to strike five. Cocktail hour. No scotch before five. That was the rule, although where that was written—on what sacred stone—Gordon couldn't say. Four was just as good as five, as far as he was concerned. But therein lay the slippery slope. A month before, he'd have fudged it to four. Three months before, he hadn't had a clock in the office, which meant it was always five o'clock. But that was when he'd been in the depths of the sleepwalker case and hitting a lot of personal lows. *Lows* was actually being generous. He was broke, heartbroken, chasing the past, and drinking heavily. Since then, things had changed.

Gordon had a girlfriend. Dana Frisco. Detective Dana Frisco. A picture of her sat just to the right of his computer, taken at Waterstones, a swanky bistro near the inner harbor just the previous month. Dana was leaning forward slightly, always eager, always engaged. Her shining black hair settled over her darkened shoulders. Her smile was fierce but friendly, and Dana could be either. Depending. Gordon's eyes were wide in the picture, and he looked nervous, as if he expected someone to jump out of the bushes to pinch him and wake him up. He'd thought of himself as *divorced* for so long that he occasionally still caught himself staring at the photo in shock, as if he was looking at another Gordon in a parallel universe.

Prior to the Waterstones photo, the only photograph in Gordon's office was a large portrait of him with his arm rested awkwardly upon the wingback chair in which Karen Jefferson, his ex-wife and still half of the nameplate of the Jefferson and Pope practice—although only in name—sat primly with her ankles crossed. Well, that picture and a yellowing four-by-six of him and his mother, Deborah, taken the last time she'd dragged him to her Laguna Beach time-share. He'd pinned it to a corkboard by the computer with other odds and ends. She looked radiant and trim at seventy-five. He looked pallid and a little ill at forty-five.

Another new addition: better reading material on top of the john. After the divorce, when Gordon was forced to give up the condo and move into his office full time for cash reasons, he took all that he owned and stuffed it into various places willy-nilly. In a fog of depression, he'd put a stack of old newspapers in the bathroom as if the prior year's *New York Times* was entertaining reading. Now, he had the most current medical journals on rotation. Probably not much better, from an entertainment standpoint, for anyone outside the profession. But at least they were current.

The new business had helped spiff up his wardrobe, replenish his scotch collection, and bring him back from the financial brink to mere low-level financial discomfort felt by the majority of single-income private-practice psychiatrists. But Dana Frisco was the real reason he'd picked himself up. She made him consider things he thought he'd never consider again after Karen—things that made his stomach do little loops that were both uncomfortable and oddly exciting, like a roller-coaster ride. Both of them were strapped in, listening to the *tik tik tik tik* of the climb—the classic kind of coaster that clacked and shook your teeth and was built on old bones. When you were on it, always in the back of your mind was the very real possibility that the entire structure, planks and nuts and bolts and all, might crumble to the ground on which it stood. Their relationship felt new and old at the same time, and it thrilled him.

But even thoughts of Dana couldn't make the clock tick to cocktail hour any faster. Nor could spinning a pencil in his hand. The only thing that could speed up that clock was creating a reason to celebrate, and Gordon had one. He'd just submitted his final approvals for his article in the fall quarterly of *Philosophy, Psychiatry, & Psychology*, Gordon's sole published contribution to the field of psychiatry to date —the result of a tireless effort to save a young boy in East Baltimore from himself. The case had changed Gordon's life and given him a burst of clients. For a man that took any excuse for a celebratory swig, that was plenty.

He popped the cork top of a very decent single malt. No more plastic bottles for him. He smelled the bouquet as he poured—a wildfire of peat that nearly made his eyes water and definitely made his mouth water. He lifted the glass to his mouth.

The phone rang. Gordon blinked in annoyance. Jefferson and Pope was closed. No calls taken after hours. For the first time in five years, Gordon could say he had a halfway decent business, so "operating hours" finally meant something. He waited out the rattling ring of his old landline then lifted his glass again. The answering machine kicked on while he took a long sip.

"Dr. Pope? Are you there?"

Gordon paused, pursing his lips, scotch between his teeth. Something in her tone of voice turned the sip sour in his mouth and pulled at his gut, not unlike a big drop on that old wooden rollercoaster.

"Please... please pick up."

And that was all it took to get Gordon to forget about the scotch. He swallowed the one sip and forwent the rest. He was almost powerless to do anything else.

That was how he found himself driving to a Marriott on Center Street with the words of a woman named Dianne West ringing in his ears: *"It's my daughter. It's hard to explain. To be honest, I don't think you'd believe me if I told you."*

GORDON SPENT ten minutes driving up and down Center Street looking for an Extended Stay Marriott, but he had no luck. He was in a swanky area of town—nothing Extended Stay about it. Then he saw the JW Marriott: sleek black marble with a glittering chandelier above the valet. Carpet on the sidewalk. Gordon wasn't about to hand over his beat-up two-seater to a place with carpet on the sidewalk. He had no cash, for one. He was making ends meet, but not *valet* making ends meet. Plus, on that block, he was fairly sure the valet just rolled cars like his into the harbor.

Fifteen minutes to find a parking spot and five more to walk. Gordon's scuffed oxfords clacked across the black marble entryway of the JW half an hour after he'd hung up with Dianne West. He nodded at the valet as if he hadn't just driven off to avoid him, and he pushed his way through the revolving doors. Two desk clerks looked up at him in unison, half smiling.

"I'm here to see a Mrs. Dianne West. My name is Gordon Pope."

The smiles became a good deal more gracious.

A trimly dressed manager seemed to appear from nowhere. He placed a brief hand upon the nearest clerk's shoulder to still her typing and said, "I'll take it from here. This way, Dr. Pope."

They walked through the marbled lobby and past the elevator bay, turned right, and walked down another, shorter hallway until they stood in front of a single elevator that opened as soon as the manager pressed the call button. Inside, he swiped a keycard and hit the top floor. They rose in silence.

When the doors opened, the manager held them with a soft press of his hand and gave a brief bow as Gordon exited. "Last on the left, Dr. Pope."

The elevator doors closed behind him. The hallway was long but had only four doors on each side. At the end was a large, rectangular window overlooking a busy intersection, yet Gordon heard nothing of the city outside. His shoes made a soft pressing sound as he walked, barely louder than kneading bread.

Gordon stopped in front of the last door on the left. He brushed his head free of the dampness that seemed to crown it every time he found himself in one of those situations, where he didn't know what was behind the door. He wiped his hands on the seat of his pants and pulled at the cuffs of his shirt. He knocked once then twice and went for a third, but the door opened with a jerk, and Gordon swiped at air.

"Dr. Pope. Thank you for coming. Dianne West. Inside, please."

A short, trim woman with a blond bob and a sharp glint in her eye grabbed his shoulder with surprising strength. Gordon was practically pulled inside. As his eyes adjusted to the low light, he saw the room was but one of several attached, a suite that sprawled to his left and right. The door closed behind him, and the first thing Gordon heard after the click and slide of the lock was a rhythmic whining, as if someone was trying to lift something heavy and failing, again and again and again. Gordon knew better.

Gordon moved immediately toward the door on the right, where the sound was coming from, but again he was stopped, spun around by Dianne.

She assayed him keenly, unblinking. "Before I let you go in there, I must be assured of your absolute discretion, Dr. Pope. I appreciate how you helped the sleepwalking children, but I heard of it from the news. I cannot have anything in the news. Understood?"

Gordon had dealt with controlling families before. He knew the only way he was going to see the girl was to agree. The rest could be sorted out later.

"I assume you're her legal guardian?" Gordon asked.

Dianne nodded.

"Then unless she's being abused, what you say goes."

Dianne still held his bicep, her eyes running over his face as if she could read it like tea leaves. Whatever she saw, it was enough. She nodded.

"Her name is Sophie. She's prone to... episodes."

Gordon turned again and walked toward the strained cries. He passed through an interior doorway into a second bedroom, and Sophie immediately went silent. Gordon looked about. He'd expected to find the girl in bed but couldn't see her anywhere. The bedspread was military tight, the glassware still covered in paper doilies. One mint rested on each of the enormous feather pillows on pillows on pillows. He glanced toward the bathroom. The sink was running, but the lights were off. Gordon made a move that way when a soft scratching on the carpet to his left gave him pause.

"Sophie?"

A single, soft moan. Clipped quickly that time. Gordon stepped past the dresser and minibar and flat-screen television and stopped at the foot of the bed. Sophie West was on the floor between the nightstand and a four-corner desk set against the wall. She had the same blond hair as her mother although hers was much longer and had a glistening, unwashed look. Her eyes were the same color of blue as well, staring straight up at Gordon. She'd stretched her plaid dress over bony knees. Her right hand was hovering over her shoes, scuffed white hush puppies. She held her fingers over the right shoe as though contemplating a chess move. The other hand she had balled into a fist, stuffed halfway into her mouth. Her backpack was open on her other side, and a set of high-quality colored pencils lay propped carefully against it, organized by color.

As soon as she saw Gordon, she started to keen continuously again. Her eyes darted to Dianne, who had followed a step behind Gordon, her hands wringing.

"Now Sophie, stop that," she said. "Can you hear me? Sophie, look at me now. This is Dr. Pope. He's here to help you."

Sophie remained unchanged. Dianne moved in toward her, but Gordon stilled her with a firm hand on one shoulder.

"Mrs. West, I have a policy," he said. "I work with children. Children alone. If you want my help, I'm going to need to work with Sophie one-on-one. Which means you out of the room."

Gordon watched her steadily. That was always a pivotal moment in patient treatment—the parental buy in. Gordon didn't need Dianne West to tell him that Sophie was having a break of some sort. That much was evident when he walked into the room. The question was: Had she called him in order to really help her child or because she thought he could give her a quick fix and get them on their way out of the private exit from the five-star hotel.

Dianne West looked at him carefully, and Gordon could tell by the tightness in her face, the way she held her jaw apart behind her closed lips—as if she wanted to scream but was keeping it in—that she was afraid. She was afraid of what was happening, and she wanted her child helped long-term. Not quick-fixed.

She nodded, turned around, and went to the door. After giving him one last look, she closed the door behind her.

Gordon let out a breath he hadn't realized he'd been keeping in. The young girl had just gone from a simple eval-uation to a patient. And good thing, too, because Gordon wasn't a quick-fix type of doctor. To Gordon, patient care was either all-in or fold.

He took a seat at the foot of the starched bed, a good five feet from the girl. She whimpered softly, her eyes rolling.

"Sophie," Gordon said, clearly and calmly.

Her eyes moved to him. So she was in the room at least, not completely inside her head. She shifted her fist in her mouth like an awkward bit of an apple. With her long, skinny legs bunched into the corner, she looked very much like a spooked animal.

"You can say what you want to say, Sophie," Gordon said. "Whatever it is, you can say it to me."

She popped her fist out, said, "You aren't safe. Nobody is. Get away from me. I'll kill you," and slammed it in again with such force that Gordon winced.

"I am safe," Gordon said. "Wherever I am is a safe place for you."

Sophie looked at him in intervals, like a bird. He could tell from her eyes that she saw him not as a stranger as much as someone who had the misfortune to be caught up within her mind.

Gordon waited patiently, his hands clasped between his knees.

Sophie dropped her hand to the floor. "Mo's back," she whispered. The girl was going through her own private emotions: her face fell, her mouth half open, her eyes sad half-moons. Then she turned to her shoes and flipped them, one over the other. She set them just so, inching the right in with her pointer finger a millimeter at a time until the backs stood perfectly aligned with each other. She popped up to standing in an instant and walked around Gordon toward the bathroom.

Gordon stayed seated. He knew that the less he moved during that type of situation, the better. Without any knowledge of Sophie's prior medical history, the best course to take would be to create a safe space and minimize sensory input. So he watched her quietly.

For the moment, Sophie seemed to have completely forgotten about him. She turned the right and left faucets of the gleaming sink to exactly the same degree. She wet her hands, nodding her head, as if keeping time in her head. She took the bar of soap and rolled it over in her hands seven times. She set it down on the dish and washed her hands free of suds for another seven nods. She carefully removed a rolled washcloth from the basket set against the mirror and patted her hands dry. She left the sink running and proceeded to touch the top of everything on the countertop one heartbeat at a time. She turned back to the door, moved into the bedroom again, and clicked the light on and off seven times until the room was dark again.

Sophie walked around Gordon, giving him a wide berth without looking at him. After sitting down in her corner once more, she looked at her fist and set it down in her lap. She sighed. Her eyes darted at the four corners of the ceiling.

"Who is Mo?" Gordon asked, as if none of her cleaning had happened.

"He's my friend. My twin. His name is Mophie, like I'm Sophie. He's also not real. He's not real. He's not real." She repeated herself like a child confronted with what she refused to believe.

"Is Mo here right now?"

Sophie shook her head. Gordon was surprised to find himself relieved. The intensity of the girl's fear was contagious.

"His voice is, though," Sophie whispered, looking at the four corners of the room again.

"What is his voice saying?"

Sophie shook her head. Her eyes welled with tears and wandered until she could blink them back in line again.

"It's okay, Sophie. You can tell me anything. It's just you and me here. No Mo—nobody else."

Sophie grabbed her knees and tucked them close then spoke into her lap. "He says the only way to keep me safe from this place is to burn it."

Her voice was strangely calm. No waver at all, as if she

were reading off of a menu in her lap. Over a decade of treating children across the spectrum couldn't save Gordon from the shiver that inched up his spine at how defeated she sounded.

Sophie swapped her shoes again, inched them forward until they were exactly even, then popped up and moved back to the bathroom. Gordon simply watched her and stayed still.

Twenty minutes and five washes later, Gordon left Sophie in her corner of the bedroom to exit to the main parlor. Dianne West was so close to the door that he bumped her upon opening it. She didn't even try to hide that she'd been eavesdropping. Gordon eyed her blankly, too lost in his thoughts to comment, then moved over to the plush couch opposite the television and sat down. His head was jammed with years and years of case studies, and in many ways, what was afflicting Sophie found precedent there. But in other equally important ways, what he'd just seen in that room stood alone. Every time he ran down a mental checklist for a surefire diagnosis, he came up lacking. She checked boxes of several conditions but left other integral boxes unticked.

Dianne did not sit down. She stood in front of him, her arms crossed, as if urging him not to get too comfortable.

"Your daughter suffers from acute obsessive-compulsive disorder," Gordon said, starting with the easiest. "That much is obvious. And I'm sure you're already aware of it."

Dianne nodded. "The hand washing, the organizing, the counting of things. She's been doing that in some form most of her life. It's actually what usually gets her out of these messes. She... counts herself calm. It's never taken this long before."

"When children exhibit obsessive-compulsive behavior,

it's often because they feel as though their lives are out of control in ways that they cannot help. So they turn to controlling whatever they can. Counting. Washing. Organizing things in their vicinity. It can become crippling, and it often worsens if left untreated. Can you think of any reason why Sophie might be feeling out of control?"

Gordon left that in the air. He stopped short of suggesting that, in almost every case, that feeling of chaotic helplessness stemmed from disruptions in the home. Dianne grasped his meaning. She pursed her mouth as if deciding whether to take offense, but a soft shuffling sound from the back room seemed to remind her that her daughter, while slightly calmer, was still not well.

"Divorce," she said simply. "My ex-husband, Simon, ran off with his personal assistant. After twelve years of marriage. But the divorce was finalized over a year ago. He's been out of the house ever since. Could that really be it?"

Gordon shrugged. "Perhaps. The mind processes trauma in its own time. Wounds can linger. And divorce, especially after such a long time, is a big rip in the fabric of what binds a household." Gordon knew firsthand how big a tear it could be. He'd been divorced after five years and it punched a huge hole in him. The stitches were only just holding, and that was less because of him and more because of Dana.

He tapped his lower lip in thought, wondering whether a divorce in the family alone could cause Sophie's behavior. Perhaps. That was certainly a piece of the greater picture, but Gordon felt it wasn't the whole. It fit, but it didn't *click*, like jamming a puzzle piece into the wrong place.

"Is that when Mo appeared? Around the time of the divorce?"

"No," Dianne said, sighing heavily. "Mophie has been

around since Sophie could talk. I thought we were rid of him a year ago. But he came back."

"Around the time of the divorce," Gordon said to himself.

Dianne tapped out time on her fingertips then nodded.

"Was it a particularly *bad* divorce?"

Dianne moved her jaw back and forth behind closed lips. "It wasn't *pleasant* by any means, but as far as these things go, no. It was quick and clean. Simon wasn't abusive, just thoughtless. He's moved on now. Doesn't seem worse for not seeing Sophie but once or twice a year."

The textbook answer was that Sophie had created Mo as a stand-in for an absent father and developed OCD as a result of shifting terrain at home. There it was. Right there. Page one of Psychiatry 101. Except that Gordon felt no click.

"I've never had an imaginary friend come back," Gordon said thoughtfully, scratching at his scruff.

"Excuse me?"

He looked up at Dianne, who stepped closer to hear him. "I've treated plenty of children with imaginary friends. And many who acted out through those friends in violent ways like burning or cutting. But once the friend goes away, I've never had one come back."

Dianne cringed. "So she told you, then. About the burning."

Gordon nodded and watched Dianne quietly. One of the most powerful weapons in his arsenal was the silent wait-out. Gordon could wait quietly better than anyone he knew. A pregnant pause made people so uncomfortable that they often offered up more than he ever could have pried from them—all of their own accord.

"We had an... incident. Some years past. When Sophie

was ten. She set fire to a good chunk of the estate, claiming Mo told her to do it."

Gordon sat back on the couch and watched Dianne carefully. "That would have been before the divorce," he said. "So Sophie has been exhibiting concerning behavior for some time."

Dianne nodded and looked away. "My daughter is recently worse. But she was... always a little off."

"Mrs. West, if I'm going to treat Sophie, I need complete honesty from you. Do you understand?"

"So that means you'll fix her?"

"In psychiatry, there are no quick fixes. Especially with children. And especially if the parents of those children aren't straight with me."

Dianne reddened and picked at the arm of the couch. Embarrassment? Anger? Either way, Gordon could tell she wasn't used to being spoken to in that way.

"I'm sorry," she said primly. "It's just that my family..." There she trailed off, carefully measuring her words. "My family is in politics. And the Baltimore political scene is notorious for taking everything they can and throwing it against you. In other cities, in other states, children would be off-limits, but not here. Do you understand what I'm saying?"

"Are you concerned for your daughter's health or your reputation?" Gordon asked, struggling to keep his voice level.

Dianne squared to Gordon. "Both," she said unabashedly.

Gordon couldn't help shaking his head. Of all the times to think of oneself...

"Can't it be both?" Dianne asked. "I promise I'll be up front with you however I can. Will you help her?"

Gordon stood. He walked to the door, but in the interval caught a glimpse into the bedroom once again. He saw a meticulously placed pair of scuffed white hush puppies and, just poking out from the corner, the toes of Sophie's stocking feet. They were curled tightly into the carpet.

Gordon was fairly sure he didn't like Dianne West, but that was nothing new. He quite frequently butted heads with the parents of his patients. Gordon wasn't going to help Sophie because Dianne asked. He was going to help her because Sophie herself couldn't ask. She was right there, but she couldn't ask. She was frightened. And she needed help.

"I'll clear my schedule," Gordon said. As if his calendar had been jammed for years and not just respectably cluttered for a matter of weeks.

CHAPTER FOUR

Dana Frisco and her daughter, Chloe, watched Gordon chew thoughtfully as he sat across the table. He cut his pork loin slowly, his eyes off in the distance. Chloe turned to her and rolled her eyes hugely, nodding at him. Dana gave a lot of credit to Chloe. Other eight-year-olds might have made a scene if their mom's eccentric new boyfriend ate his dinner without speaking. She knew he wasn't deliberately being rude. His mind was just elsewhere. He ate like a placid cow. An enlightened placid cow, but a cow nonetheless.

Dana cleared her throat. "Earth to Gordon. Are you with us, Gordon?"

Gordon looked over at her. "Hmm?"

"The salt, big guy. Chloe asked for the salt. Three times."

"Oh." Gordon fumbled to set his knife and fork down. Then he fumbled again with the salt, spilling a cascade Chloe's way, which elicited another eye roll that would have held its own against even the most jaded teenagers. Dana would know. As one of two detectives in the newly formed

Child Protective Investigations unit of the Baltimore Police Department, she'd been dealing with a lot of teenagers lately. She'd found, even in the month she'd been assigned the detail, that teenagers rolled their eyes at just about everything, good or bad.

"Chloe, keep your eyes in your head," Dana said.

By all rights, her daughter should have another four years before the serious cynicism set in. Then again, Chloe had always been ahead of her class. And really, she couldn't blame the girl. Gordon was awkward around Chloe in the best of circumstances. He seemed to settle right in with all the new kids he was getting as patients, but you'd never know it the way he acted around her daughter—which was a bit like an awkward butler.

Gordon set about muttering apologies and gathering the salt with his palm until he accidentally dumped all of it down a seam in the table. He paused as it hit the floor. Beets, her mother's Boston terrier, was there in a flash, tongue to wood flooring. Gordon gave up and handed Chloe the salt. She managed not to shake her head as she put a tad too much of it on her mashed potatoes, which Dana chalked up as a parenting victory.

"Where's your head at today?" Dana asked.

"It's here. It really is."

Dana gathered a bite on her fork. "Work gets to me too. It's okay."

Gordon cleared his throat. "A tough patient came in. A strange case. Very strange."

"Strange?" asked Dana.

Gordon glanced at Chloe, who was watching Beets go to town and looked like she couldn't care less.

"Strange behavioral markers. There's an obvious obsessive-compulsive diagnosis, but... it just doesn't fit well. It's hard to explain."

Beets ran his bulk into Gordon's shin in search of more salt.

"Hey, Chloe..." Gordon said.

She looked up in wary surprise.

"Did you ever have an imaginary friend?"

Chloe thought. "No."

"What about Bun Bun?" Dana said. "Remember Bun Bun?"

Chloe reddened a hint. "That was nothing. Just me talking to my Bun Bun stuffed animal is all. I don't do it anymore."

"Why not?" Gordon asked.

The genuine, almost childlike curiosity in his voice seemed to give Chloe pause.

"I dunno. I got real friends like Alex and Catelyn. Not so much Catelyn. But for sure Alex."

Gordon nodded absently, clearly lost in thought once again.

"I still like Bun Bun, though," Chloe added, as if she felt guilty. "Even though I don't play with him anymore. He's on my favorite shelf and stuff, still."

Dana heard a telltale shuffling sound from just downstairs, where her mother was supposedly "watching her shows." Dana's house was small, but she knew the downstairs television was farther away than the base of the stairs. She heard her mother clear her throat and barely stopped herself from rolling her own eyes.

"Yes, Mama?" Dana said loudly.

"Chloe, it's time to finish your schoolwork," Maria Frisco said loudly, as if Dana hadn't spoken.

Chloe looked at Dana with all her might until Dana eventually nodded that Chloe could be excused. She jumped up and clattered her dishes to the sink, where she stood on her tiptoes to run some perfunctory water over the lot before setting them loudly in the basin. Then she shot off down the stairs.

The dining room was quiet.

"She has candy down there," Dana said.

Gordon picked morosely at what was left on his plate. "Candy?"

"Ma keeps a huge jar of Starbursts in her room. She's been spoiling Chloe since she could walk. It's nothing personal. Plus, her toys are down there."

"So she's not really doing homework."

"I doubt it."

"So not only does Chloe think I'm weird, but your mom doesn't want me around her to begin with."

Dana let out an even breath. That was about the whole of it. She wouldn't lie to the man. Gordon nodded. She could see he was trying to shrug off the double dismissal as no big deal but only partly succeeding.

"I get it. And I know I don't have a lot to talk about with Chloe. I just... I think I'm still trying to figure all this out, and kids always know."

"What are you trying to figure out?" Dana asked, a hint of worry tingeing her voice. She knew he cared for her, but she sometimes wondered if all this—her daughter, her mother, her job—could ever find space in the brain of a man like Gordon Pope. A brain that was already filled to the brim.

"I'm terrified that all this could fall apart, at any second," Gordon said. "It's all so fragile. Everything is. You see some of the kids I've seen—you see how they're shattered. They're just shattered." His face dropped, and he was clearly thinking of something recent. Something fresh. Something today. "And they don't know why, you know? You can break inside even if you don't know why. Your brain doesn't care if you understand why it's falling apart. If it's gonna fall apart, it'll do it regardless. Sometimes the deck is stacked against you no matter what you do. And sometimes I get afraid the deck is stacked against me too. Against us."

Dana stood and walked over to him and plucked him up from his seat by the crook of one arm. She turned him to face her.

"Gordon, the reason you're good at what you do is because you get in the heads of these kids. You become them. But these kids are damaged. Don't forget that. Don't let them damage you."

Gordon wasn't tall, but she was shorter. Still, she pulled him close. He came reluctantly at first, like a teen being dragged onto a dance floor. Eventually he nuzzled low into her neck and hung there.

"Your mother hates me," he said.

"She's old-school Catholic. She saw what it did to Chloe and me when Brett left. Right now, she hates everyone not me or Chloe. And occasionally, just everyone not Chloe."

He let her hold him for a time, fully there with her at last, before saying, "I should go."

"I'm on night shift, but I'll try to come over late night."

Gordon nodded, already falling back into his own mind again, as he had with the last "strange case" he'd come across. The sound of Chloe laughing downstairs gave Gordon a brief, bittersweet look. Dana knew that every attempt he'd made at getting Chloe to laugh had fallen flat—nothing but eye rolls in return.

"Her toys are all down there..." Dana offered, again.

He shrugged on his jacket and placed a hand on her shoulder. "It's okay. Kids come around in their own time," he said. "If they think it's worth it."

She watched as he pulled away in that rattling car of his, one brake light out, some internal belt whining softly. His off-key horn bopped twice in farewell.

That night, Dana went through her open cases file by file while her mother watched a movie with Chloe—the same Disney movie she'd watched earlier that week, by the sound of it. And several times the week before. Chloe's voice squeaked in off-key beauty, every word on cue as if she was reading from a karaoke machine. Her grandma would be bobbing along, clapping her hands softly on her knees. The thought made Dana smile, which was good. It almost offset the melancholy that settled over her every time she cracked a file folder recently.

She'd thought making detective would change everything, and in many ways it had. She made more. She got the badge. She got off the beat and into a new department she thought would be the perfect fit. But the more things changed, the more they stayed the same.

She thought the detail change meant that she'd also leave her old boss, Warren Duke, behind—that she'd be able to start fresh in a department not run by an entitled, blue-blooded lieutenant hell-bent on keeping everyone not in his inner circle "where they're best suited." That, in her case, meant *in her place*.

She should have known better. CPI didn't fall under Lieutenant Duke's jurisdiction. However, it did fall under *Major* Duke's jurisdiction. A district is a lot of territory— hard not to fall inside that. Too much to hope that she'd be promoted out. She'd helped crack a major case. With police, the shit rolled downhill, good and bad. When she was recognized, he was recognized too.

So there went that. Exit plan foiled. Window slammed shut. The thought made her throat itch, as though she'd swallowed a pill wrong and a little piece of it had lodged somewhere below her neck and above her lungs.

As if being under Duke's thumb wasn't bad enough, the work itself in her new detail was completely underwhelming. She thought CPI would put her in the middle of cases with teeth—things like abductions, gang recruitment, trafficking, abuse—but the cases she saw came from Duke, and she and Gordon had beaten Duke at his own game with the sleepwalkers case. She quickly learned Duke didn't take well to getting beaten at his own game.

Dana flipped through her tabs again, each finger-worn by then. She had twelve open cases. Six of them were repeat truancies. Four were petty vandalism. Two were social-work assists—validating food stamps. Never one to sit and take it on the chin, Dana had already spoken to Duke. As one of two detectives in a new unit commissioned by the mayor himself, she could still do that—go to the major and act while she still had favor on her side. So she asked for any one of the myriad of cases she knew were out there in homicide or CSI involving youth. Cases that might be better served with her.

Duke never even looked up from his paperwork when he told her to "enter the pool slowly." So there went that.

Chloe warbled out a verse of song from the basement that broke Dana's melancholy. She eased her grip on the file in front of her, which she'd been subconsciously crushing. Truancy cases only got so much traction—kids who didn't want to go to school wouldn't go to school. What Dana wanted was a case where a kid wanted to go to school but couldn't. Those existed, she was sure of it. But in the BPD, you tackled the case that crossed your desk, no matter what department you were in. Dana rubbed her eyes and checked the clock—well past Chloe's bedtime once again.

She took Chloe through her bedtime ritual with as much vigor as she could muster. Chloe had a singing toothbrush on its last legs that sounded a bit like a phone call under water, but Dana sang along nonetheless, brushing side by side with her daughter. She read her favorite bedtime story to her for the third time that week, about a teddy bear named Mr. Buttons, who loses his felt nose.

"Mr. Buttons walked a long path through the forest every day. And every day, Mr. Buttons tapped the trees with his felt nose so he could find his way..."

She turned on Chloe's night-light. The mobile of stars above her bed lit her small bedroom glowworm green. Then Dana went to her own bed and lay down fully clothed on top of the puffy duvet she ended up kicking off every night, feeling vaguely disappointed in everything without being able to pinpoint why.

Dana shot awake in darkness—she froze, disoriented and with a ringing in her ears. Many hammered heartbeats later, she was finally able to place herself: on top of her bedspread, still in her clothes. She must have fallen asleep where she'd lain.

Her neck was damp around the collar, her pants bunched at the legs. The ringing persisted. She shook her head to clear it, to no effect, until she realized it was coming from her purse. She stared dumbly at the glow of her phone while she pulled it out. Its screen lit the entire room and read "Marty Cicero." Her partner.

"Hey Marty," she answered, trying to sound alert.

"Wakey wakey," Marty said, his shipyard east-coast

accent punching through the phone. Eighties hair metal was blaring in the background: Marty's unique way of dusting his own cobwebs. "We got a crime scene."

DANA AND MARTY had been partners before CPI. They were assigned together to the beat by Warren Duke, who often threw hard-case cops at Dana like a kid lording over a science set, just to see what came of it. To see who survived. In the end, Dana was always standing. If surviving meant staying right where she was while the men who sat beside her in the cruiser moved out and up, then she was the definition of a survivor, but that's all she did: survive. Then Marty came around, the first beat partner she didn't immediately want to throttle, despite how he sometimes came off like a gym rat. Since then, she'd had plenty of opportunities to see that he was much more than his meathead exterior. He was fiercely loyal and more perceptive than anyone in the department, save herself. They'd become friends and developed a strong rapport. She knew Marty wanted more, a partnership of a different kind. He'd all but confessed himself to her when they broke the sleepwalkers case, but so far she'd been able to avoid the topic directly. The new detail helped. Both of them were still trying to tread water, finding their place again. That took up most of their time. Eventually, however, she knew they'd settle in, and things would need to be addressed.

Marty knew she cared deeply for Gordon, but he was also stubborn, refusing to back down even in the face of defeat. She wanted desperately to keep things working between them. And between Marty and Gordon, who had a frosty relationship, to say the least, although Marty was most often the antagonist. Gordon was too oblivious in many ways—too single-minded in others—to have much of a frosty relationship with anyone. Except when people stepped between him and his patients.

So much for seeing Gordon that night. He would understand.

From what Dana had gathered on the phone, the case was their first big one. Felony destruction of property was a big deal. She felt more and more like a police detective as she dressed. Then she tried her best to tiptoe past Chloe's room and left a note under Maria's door. They knew the drill. Back on the beat, Dana was often out more nights than in.

She felt strange driving to a crime scene in her minivan, but she didn't have time to report to the station. The van was a relic of the old days with Brett, back when she'd thought Chloe would be one of at least two, maybe three. Maybe even four. If things kept going the way she thought they were going to with Gordon, Chloe would likely be her last. She didn't know the first thing about adoption, and Gordon was sterile. The minivan had a lot of empty seats. Sometimes, when she looked in the rearview mirror, she felt as if she was looking into a bare closet, and she was nudged by a hollow sadness. But it was a good car. It was as sturdy as a tank, and it just kept running, so she ran with it—empty seats and all.

She plugged in the directions Marty had given her and took off, cruising north past the city, then past the suburbs, into neighborhoods that looked less like neighborhoods and more like well-kept hedge mazes with houses hidden inside. Her tires hissed down a newly paved two-lane road, and she slowed to the speed limit only when she saw the turnoff in the distance. An enormous ivy-clad gate met her at Merryville. Not Merryville Estates or Merryville Place or

Merryville Manors—just Merryville. The name was written on an oxidized brass plaque attached to a redbrick guard station. An attendant stepped from the station at the sound of her approach—an older man in a maroon jacket and slacks with a green tie. He carried a clipboard and watched her benignly over spectacles perched on the tip of his nose. The clock on Dana's dash read 2:08 in the morning.

"May I have your name, ma'am?" the attendant asked.

"Dana Frisco. Detective Dana Frisco," she added, after a moment.

"May I see your badge, please?"

Dana unclipped her shield from her hip and brought out her identification. The attendant looked at both carefully. Back up at her. Back to the pad. Then to her badge again. Dana tapped the side of her car and looked beyond the gate. Somewhere in the distance, lights were flashing silent red and blue, a lot of them. But the trees were too dense to figure out where.

"Straight ahead, ma'am," the attendant said. "Just down Long Lane." He handed back her badge. The gate swung open smoothly. The moonlight caught the ivy as it moved, the leaves fluttering briefly in the still night air. They'd turned yellow and red in a swath on the diagonal, like flung paint.

Dana drove in silence down a wide avenue flanked at even intervals by towering white oak trees. The houses she saw beyond the trees sometimes spanned half a block. Each had a big main, often an imposing plantation-looking building, but most houses had other houses—at least one, maybe two. Like ducks in a row. She saw lights on in some of the windows, despite the hour. Faces in silhouette, like small black dots, peeked out. One man in a long robe stood boldly on his front porch, eyeing her. *They must not see a lot of flashing lights here.*

She crawled by—even if she'd had lights and sirens, they would be off and quiet. She was part of an investigatory unit, so Dana and Marty arrived in the aftermath now. They pieced together the scene after others had put out the fires.

The moon dappled the road through the leaves as Dana rounded a soft bend, then slowed.

Unless the "fire" is actually a fire.

A stalwart-looking redbrick structure was belching smoke darker than the night from its ground-floor windows. Dana couldn't see any flames, but the building still glowed an angry red inside. Two firefighters were handling a hose to keep a steady stream of water jetting into the nearest window. Six or seven others milled around, speaking to each other, standing with arms crossed. By their relaxed body language, Dana could tell the blaze was under control. Time for the detectives, which begged the question: Why call CPI?

Marty was waiting behind the trucks, leaning against his Charger and munching on his ever-present bag of almonds like popcorn at the movie theater. He wore a polo shirt that looked painted onto his broad frame, dark denim jeans, and high-top basketball shoes. His badge hung from a dog-tag chain around his neck and rested between his pecs. He looked as fresh as a morning bird. Dana looked briefly down at her own clothes, workout pants and whatever T-shirt had been on top of the pile. She made a mental note to put together some sort of outfit for times like that and set it away on top of the dresser. She needed to look like a cop, not a harried mom trying to squeeze in five minutes on the treadmill.

Marty held out the almonds to her as she approached. "Brain food," he said. "Low calorie, high payoff." He looked her up and down and smiled but kept quiet.

Dana yawned and took a handful. She leaned back on the gleaming hood next to Marty, and both of them took in the scene. Two uniformed police walked the perimeter, speaking with curious neighbors as they approached, keeping others away.

They crunched almonds in comfortable silence.

"I don't get it," Dana said. "Why call us in?"

Marty pointed at whitewashed wooden lettering sticking out from a flowering hedge across the road, just offset from the building: Merryville Preparatory Academy - Est. 1893.

"I get that it's a high school," Dana said. "We got that much from dispatch."

"Everything school," Marty said, his accent pinging off the words. "One of those baby-kids-through-high-school deals."

"Baby kids?"

"Yeah, like two, three years old. I asked."

"So day care through high school. You work for a child-protection unit, Marty. You gotta talk shop."

Marty shrugged. "Eh. They're all kids to me," Marty said, not unkindly.

Dana was still trying to figure out precisely how Marty felt about kids as both of them settled into their new jobs. He had none of his own, and at first glance he was the type of guy who might hold out a baby at arm's length, blinking dumbly, traps bulging. But he'd surprised Dana with how comfortable he was around Chloe. The few times they'd met, he spoke to her like an old friend, getting down to her level. Chloe still talked about the time he'd given her a handful of confetti poppers at the barbecue Dana hosted to celebrate their promotions.

"They think a kid did this?" Dana asked.

"I think they want to rule it out. Although I'm not too sure what they think we're gonna find after it's been hosed down and picked through by the first responders."

Marty nodded toward where two other policemen were listening patiently as a group of men and women were all trying to speak over one another.

"I think this might be one of those 'call in the cavalry to shut up the rich people' type deals." He popped another almond in his mouth and chewed around a smile. "They had to punch through a Land Rover to get to the hydrant across the street. Ran the hose right through the windows and over the steering wheel. It was awesome."

Dana suppressed a smile. "Let's start at the back. Away from those people."

One of the uniformed police—a sleepy-looking young guy from nearby Bolger station—told her the easiest place to start was with the head of janitorial services. He pointed out a slightly stooped older man in an oil-stained canvas jacket and sharply creased work slacks. Dana flashed him her badge and pulled him from the minor scrum forming near the hamstrung Land Rover. He didn't need much persuading.

"Security cameras show somebody coming in from the west entrance just before the fire." He handed Dana an eight-by-eleven print, in black and white, time-stamped at 12:17 a.m., barely two hours before.

The picture was grainy and off-center, taken from above. It showed a small person walking down a darkened hallway, not much taller than the surrounding lockers. The figure wore light pants—probably jeans—and a white T-shirt. A black baseball hat obscured the face and head.

"This is all we got," he said. "The kid kept away from the cameras, which is why we think they knew the place. That and it's a pretty private neighborhood. Not a lot of outsiders."

"West side's as good a place as any to start," Dana said.

The janitor talked as they walked, in a voice that sounded scratched by cigarettes. "West side is the main entrance. The school was a manor house for most of the eighteen hundreds. Way too big for its own good. East side was added later. It's where the science labs are. That's what was torched."

They followed the man down an immaculately kept walkway that wound around the building to the west.

"How much does this school cost for a kid?" Marty asked, his head on a swivel.

The janitor sniffed and shook his head slightly. "Twenty thousand a year, to start."

Marty laughed. "Twenty thousand a year for high school?"

The janitor shook his head. "No, son. Twenty thousand for elementary. To start. High school is thirty-two thousand a year. And going up. If you can get a spot. And you don't need to tell me how crazy that is. I already know."

Marty whistled. With the way the janitor spoke—the shake of his head—if Dana were to guess, she would say he made about as much for a year of work as one of these high-school kids paid to attend. Maybe less.

"Here you go," he said as they came upon wide wooden double doors under darkened metal sconces. He unlocked the doors and heaved them open, ushering them inside the main foyer. At that end, the school was silent. Their shoes squeaked softly on the floor, an enormous tiled mosaic of the school crest, which depicted a flaming torch over an open door surrounded by Latin. The janitor stopped them at the center and pointed at a gleaming glass eye nestled in an upper corner of the ceiling, pointing down the right hallway of lockers.

"That's the camera that caught the kid. He went down the hallway there, toward the east wing. And this is where I'll leave you. I suspect I gotta start cleaning what they'll let me on the east side. We're already gonna be shut down long enough as it is. Let me know when you're done. I gotta lock up again. Fire or no fire, I gotta lock up."

Dana thanked him, and he nodded, already looking distracted by his own thoughts as he walked back out. The heavy double doors softly clicked shut behind him.

A single line of emergency halogen lights buzzed overhead, snaking from all directions toward the various exits. The fire-alert strobes still pulsed even though the alarm had long since been silenced.

"Hello?" Marty shouted.

Dana winced involuntarily as his voice echoed down the halls and off the lockers. She looked at him skeptically.

Marty shrugged. "Never hurts to check."

They both set off down the east hall, toward the fire, following a path already tracked and slightly wet from the firefighters. They walked slowly and in silence, and with each step away from the main foyer, the air seemed to darken. Dana found herself squinting to make out the locker numbers and was patting at her pockets for a light when she heard a soft, metallic tap and ring, like the sound of a dropped coin that then rolls.

Both detectives froze.

The sound had come from somewhere ahead of them, beyond the safety lights, in the pitch blackness.

"You heard that, right?" Dana whispered.

Marty nodded.

She strained her eyes but saw no movement. The hall gaped like a long, empty highway under a covered moon. Dana's hand ventured to her gun, in a holster under her arm, but she hesitated. Drawing a gun in a school felt wrong when a kid might be on the other end of it. "You bring a flashlight?" she asked instead.

Marty let out a sigh just loud enough for her to hear then put a small Maglite in her hand with a wry smile. He turned on his own massive Maglite.

"What would you do without me?" he asked.

"Walk around in the dark in peace." She rolled her eyes.

Together, they made their way slowly down the hall, beams of light sweeping the floors and walls, reflecting off the glass windows of the closed classroom doors. Several steps later, Marty pressed lightly on Dana's arm. His beam fell in an expanding line down the left-side lockers, blocks of dull green metal, each shut as tight as the next—save one.

They watched the open door of the locker for a moment. Dana could have sworn it was moving when the beams first caught it, swinging halfway closed. It occurred to her that if it had swung open and into the next locker door, it might have sounded something like a dropped and rolling coin.

Dana called out, "Hello?"

She strained her ears, listening for anything, which meant she heard everything—the revving of the fire trucks' diesel engines as they moved about, the ringing of the halogen safety lights above—but also things that might not be there, that might be her brain tricking her. The distant hum of traffic or a scampering down in the darkness? The first responders talking back and forth somewhere outside, or a muffled laugh, small and childish? Dana shook her head as though she had water in her ears. She couldn't be sure what she heard.

Marty walked over to the open locker, gave the door a perfunctory swing until it tapped the one next to it. The sound was remarkably similar. He lit up the inside. All Dana could see was trash. Lined notebook paper crumpled into balls, maybe ten of them, lay at the bottom. He sifted through them with his flashlight then moved to the small cubby up top, and there he stopped.

"What is it?" she asked.

He moved aside, his face vaguely confused. "Take a look."

Dana stepped in, shining her light. There, in the otherwise empty cubby, was the only flat piece of paper in the locker. Dana started to reach for it before she saw it was a picture drawn in colored pencil. She turned her head to match the orientation. At a glance, it looked like a black dinner table surrounded by fire. Three people crouched underneath the table, out of the flame, their knees drawn to cover their faces. The artwork wasn't exactly crude—the figures were defined and shadowed and the fire well blended—but it still held an air of childishness to it, multiple lines to sketch the bodies, the coloring uneven and scribbled at the edges.

A boy stood on top of the table, legs spread, hands on hips as if it was a podium and he'd just won gold. His smile was a half-moon sliver slit with lines for teeth. A black baseball cap's brim poked out at an odd angle from his head

"We oughta bag this," Dana said quietly.

A year before, Dana knew that Marty might have

second-guessed her. Procedure was to take in the scene, establish your fundamentals about how things should be, then look for things that didn't fit. A bunch of scribbled trash in an open locker? He'd have said it was no big deal. But that was then. Now, Marty took out a bag. He picked up the drawing with a pinched kerchief from his pocket, sealed it, and carefully tucked it flat in his back pocket. After a moment's hesitation, he picked up a crumpled piece from the bottom and unfolded it.

"Same picture, more or less," he said.

"Leave them. If they mean anything, we'll come back. They'll keep."

Dana noted the locker number, 210, then moved on down the hall, Marty close behind. She stepped carefully and quietly and replayed her first glance down the hallway in her mind, along with the sound she'd heard.

"Did you see anyone?" she whispered.

"No. But I definitely heard something."

They reached the end of the hallway, where it formed a T at what looked to be the library, locked tight. To the right were more darkened lockers and a double-door exit, barely illuminated. To the left, the hall sloped slightly downward, toward the fire. Dana cocked her head in the direction of the darkened exit and focused on listening. She shone her light down the hall, where its beam died twenty feet out. The red exit sign glowed like an evil eye. Not a sound that way. She turned around. Marty was flashing his light perfunctorily through the windows of the locked library, where it refracted and scattered around the cut glass.

"C'mon," she said. "Let's get to the scene."

When Marty swung his light to the left, something caught Dana's eye. The light-blue walls of the school were painted with a racing stripe of the school's colors, crimson and white, but the white was marked. The effect was faint, especially in the low light, but it was noticeable. An erratic scribble of orange leveled out into a dragged streak, as if someone had walked alongside the wall with a pencil stuck out at their side.

Dana followed the orange down the hall as it leveled out into the east wing, and the smell of old smoke tickled her nose. Marty followed her in silence, adding his light to hers. The pencil wasn't hard to follow, a steady streak of orange, sometimes darkening with what appeared to be a nearly gouging force. Something about the colored streak reminded Dana of breadcrumbs and dark forests, as if they were meant to follow it.

In the stories, Hansel and Gretel nearly ended up in an oven. Had Dana and Marty followed the orange a few hours earlier, they would have ended up in an inferno of a different kind. As it was, their path led into the waterlogged science wing, the walls still flashing blue and red. Everything reeked of soaked ash. The orange mark looked to have been blown off by a strafing of the fire hose that broke the floor-to-ceiling windows separating the labs from the outer hallway. She could see all the way through the labs and out the big double doors in the back, which had either been removed or broken off. A fireman just outside looked at her questioningly until she flashed her badge, then he nodded and continued straightening the main hose, prepping it for rolling up.

Looking at the lab, Dana was taken back to her own high-school science classes. High black-topped tables were spaced evenly about, each with silver gas spigots to attach Bunsen burners, the only things still standing where they should—and only because they were bolted down. The cabinets for equipment that ringed the room were shattered, their contents strewn. Beakers and mixers and boxes of pipettes were scattered on the ground, their delicate glass shattered as easily as broken light bulbs. Stools that had likely ringed the tables during class were instead blown over and pushed back, even into the hallway in some cases, all casualties of the hose. Dana had responded to many fires in her time. Fire damaged. Water destroyed.

She noticed the gas levers were all turned to different angles. The air still smelled vaguely of rotten eggs, underneath the wet ash. "The burners started the fire."

Marty nodded. "What a mess," he said. "What the hell are we supposed to do with this? Read the ashes?"

Marty was right. Whatever clues the kid may have left were washed away. "We're not getting anything else from this room," she said.

Dana turned back toward the hallway they'd followed, looking at where the orange pencil stopped. Perhaps it wasn't leading inward at all. After Black Hat turned on the burners and sparked the fire, maybe he drew a trail behind him on his way out.

"Let's get some fresh air," Dana said, stepping carefully around the shattered and dripping classroom. She walked through the broken doors at the rear, joining the first responders once again. She continued past the noise, past the lights, past the bickering neighbors, all the way to Marty's car—a full loop. Both detectives leaned against the driver's side door. Marty took out his almonds. Dana let out a small sigh. She tried to piece together some sort of narrative that might fit with what they'd found in the locker, but she couldn't. She felt the picture was important, though. She felt it was something that mattered.

A man in a rumpled suit spotted them from the small crowd still near the Land Rover. His eyes settled on Marty's badge. He excused himself from a spirited debate about when the school would reopen and trudged over to them with weary, dragging steps. "Detectives?"

Dana nodded. "Dana Frisco." She extended a hand. "This is my partner, Marty Cicero. We're with the Child Protective Investigations unit."

"Jack Pence. I'm the principal." As he moved in to shake their hands, it became clear that his blue blazer was on top of pajamas. "What a mess. At least nobody was hurt. I saw you take a walk through already. Anything stand out?"

"Maybe," Dana said. "What can you tell us about the kid in the hat?" She held up the security still.

Pence nodded as if he'd stared at it for hours already, to no avail. "Already told the police and anyone that would listen. I have no idea who that is. Nobody could tell with the hat and whatnot. We have uniforms here. Nobody wears jeans and T-shirts."

"Maybe you could start from the beginning. Who called in the fire?"

"Our groundskeeper lives on site, in a small cottage in the south fields. He was the one who first saw the flames, he says around one in the morning. I got the call not long after. Probably the same time as you. That's all I know. I've been fielding questions from parents ever since. All of them are convinced this is going to throw off the graduation schedule and impact their precious snowflakes' chances at Harvard. Meanwhile, half the damn school is on fire." He pinched the bridge of his nose as if to calm himself. "I'm sorry. I wish I could be of more help."

"Any of the neighbors see anything weird?" Marty asked.

"This is a reactionary neighborhood, Detective. They wouldn't take well to seeing that picture you're holding. It means their gates and hedges aren't as bulletproof as they like to believe. Please tell me you've found something, anything, that can close this as soon as it was opened."

Dana nodded to Marty, who took the bagged drawing from his pocket.

"Anything about this strike you? We found it in an open locker. There were more like it balled up at the bottom."

At first, Dana thought Pence might dismiss the drawing. In truth, she could count on both hands the number of cases she'd investigated so far as a detective with CPI. She was still in that hazy, treacherous no-man's-land that came with a new position. If Pence laughed the drawing off as ridiculous, she'd probably believe him. That vulnerability annoyed her. Dana wanted to be good at her job right then, as good as she'd been on the beat.

"What locker?" he asked instead. He turned the bag at different angles in the light of Marty's flashlight.

"The wing of lockers just to the right of the foyer. We're going to need to know who has locker two hundred and ten."

"The two hundred block? That can't be right. Those lockers have all been cleared. We're refinishing that entire wing. A gift from the graduating class. They've been empty for two months."

Dana leaned back wearily against the car. No answers. More questions. The case hung open and swinging, as surely as locker two hundred and ten.

Pence turned his head toward another gathering clump of neighbors, and his slight sigh betrayed his annoyance.

"If you'll excuse me," Pence said, "this looks like it's going to be a long night, and it's only just started."

Dana was thinking the exact same thing.

CHAPTER FIVE

S ophie looked completely worn out. Gordon knew that
after an attack of mania often came depression, or
bone-weary exhaustion, as if the body had been drained
beyond health—similar, in many ways, to what ampheta-
mines did to the brain, firing dopamine receptors beyond
their pay grade and going negative in the vacation bank. She
seemed sore. She kept rolling her neck, tapping her sneakers
on the shaggy rug of his office, and jiggling her bony knees
as if trying to keep herself awake. Gordon tried to remember
if her knees had been so bruised two days ago at the hotel.
He couldn't recall.

"Do you remember when I came to visit you in the hotel
room, Sophie?" Gordon asked.

"A little," Sophie said.

She looked at him in fits and starts, like a bird. She sat in
his small chair, an exact replica of the one Gordon himself sat
in across from her, just slightly diminished to fit his clientele.
She smoothed the thick rug beneath her feet with the toe of
one shoe after disrupting it with the other. Smoothing, then

disrupting. Smoothing. Disrupting. When she wasn't looking at the floor or sidelong at Gordon, she looked toward the closed door to the waiting room beyond, where Dianne sat, coughing every now and then in what Gordon thought was a conspicuous manner, as if she wanted to let him know she was still there. Still a part. Still the one that had the final say.

"You were organizing some stuff. And washing your hands. Remember that?"

Sophie nodded. "I do that," she said. "Mom tells me it's silly. After a while."

Gordon noted that but didn't respond to it. "What's going through your mind when you're washing your hands and organizing your shoes? How do you feel?"

"Like if I don't, bad things will happen. Like I'm keeping bad things from happening."

"What things?"

Sophie shrugged and rolled her neck. "Dying. Getting taken. You know, bad things. They can happen to anyone. To me. To Mom. Especially girls."

"And organizing, cleaning, putting your things away the right way, these keep the bad things at bay?"

Sophie looked at Gordon for her longest stint yet. She nodded. "That and drawing."

Gordon remembered the colored pencils at her feet in the hotel room, organized by shade of color. "And what about fire?" he asked.

Sophie looked away again. Outside, Dianne cleared her throat. Gordon made a mental note to put the waiting-room furniture away from the shared wall. He felt as though Dianne had an ear pressed to the door.

"Fire's when nothing else works. Fire works then."

"Fire works for what?"

"When nothing else will save me or Mom or anyone else. Fire will."

"Save you from the bad things? Like dying or getting kidnapped?"

A sinking feeling had settled in the pit of Gordon's stomach ever since he'd left the hotel room. As Sophie spoke, it threatened to creep up and sour his throat. He cleared his throat to fight it back down, but he still couldn't shake it, and he was starting to see why. He'd assumed the fire starting was a result of the OCD symptoms, that when one of Sophie's patterns was broken, she set fire to the whole thing to "clean" it. Lashing out in that way had plenty of precedent in literature, but it wasn't a diagnosis that sat well with Gordon, and he thought he knew why.

Gordon was beginning to believe that both the fire starting and Sophie's OCD were symptoms in and of themselves, of something much more problematic.

"Sophie," Gordon said, stirring the girl, who seemed almost asleep. "Can you talk to me about Mo?"

Sophie blinked as if trying to force herself back awake. Gordon noticed, unsettlingly, that her eyes flitted to the four corners of the room once more before settling on him again, just as they had in the hotel room.

"He doesn't exist," Sophie said, as if reading a script.

"Maybe not with you and your mom. But with you and me, if he exists, he exists."

Sophie took her shoes off and set them carefully underneath the chair before tucking her feet underneath herself. She sized Gordon up as if for the first time. In Gordon's experience, first visits with kids often went in the same initial direction. They viewed appointments as a chance either to get away from their parents and act out in a new environment or to be extremely bored and sleep—until something sparked them and they realized that Gordon wasn't a babysitter. That he was, in fact, there to try to figure something out *with* them.

"He doesn't exist," Sophie said again, but her eyes said otherwise.

"Okay," Gordon said, playing along. "So he doesn't exist now. But maybe you could tell me about the first time you met him? Way back when."

Sophie rubbed her eyes, and they opened a shade brighter. "I don't remember the first time I met him. He was always sort of there. I just remember the first time I talked to him."

"Yeah? What did you guys talk about?"

"I was seven." She looked up, thinking. "No, eight. And I was feeling bad, you know. Just like something bad was coming for Mom and Dad. They were fighting and stuff before they got divorced. But that wasn't it. Even before they started fighting, I felt it coming. Just, like, I knew something bad was gonna happen, and Mo and I used to play this stupid hide-and-seek game. Which was basically me just hiding and playing with myself." Sophie shook her head, as if ashamed.

"A lot of kids have imaginary friends, Sophie. It's nothing to be ashamed of."

Sophie wasn't buying it. Her porcelain complexion was reddening. She might as well have been talking about wetting the bed. She was at an age when kids tried their hardest to distance themselves from everything that makes them kids. But Sophie couldn't distance herself from Mo.

"I'd hide, and Mo would try to find me," Sophie said. "A lot of times, I'd hide, and he'd never find me because I had a place in the basement, underneath this table, that he didn't know about."

Gordon searched for fear in Sophie's voice, but all he heard was an edge of competitiveness, almost like a sibling rivalry.

"The first time he talked was when he found me there. I was hiding where it was dark. Quiet. I felt like things weren't pressing down so much on me. Then I heard his steps. They were always light, barefoot. But I could hear them."

Gordon furrowed his brow. That was a strangely specific detail for an imaginary friend to exhibit.

"It was totally dark, but I could hear Mo moving around, giggling. Which was weird, because he'd never giggled before. And I didn't like it. So I moved to the back of the wall, but I think he heard me. Everything in the basement was real quiet, and I could hear the pipes ticking and stuff, then he stuck his face down from up top. Everything sort of caved in on me. It felt like everyone was about to die. I was about to die, too. So I curled up and closed my eyes, and that's when he said, 'Burn it.'"

"And that was the night of the fire?" Gordon asked, keeping all judgment from his voice.

Sophie nodded. "I don't remember setting it. All I remember is waking up in the hospital. Just like waking up at the hotel room."

Gordon nodded. A new diagnosis was forming. A flimsy one. Gordon wasn't happy about it—he didn't like flimsy—but it held up if what Sophie was saying was true.

"What's Mo like?" Gordon asked. "What does he look like?"

"He's just like me, but a boy. He wears dirty jeans and a messy T-shirt and stuff like he just got back from playing tag for hours, and he doesn't wear shoes. And he wears a black hat. And he smiles all the time."

Gordon's diagnosis took another whack. Those details were remarkable.

"And does he still talk to you?"

Sophie looked into her chapped hands, seeming suddenly weighed down. She'd been remarkably engaging so far, given what she'd gone through. That was a good sign —it meant she knew she had a problem and wanted it fixed —but it also took a lot out of her. He felt he didn't have much time left with her that session, before she sank under again.

"He still talks," she said. "He talked in the hotel room."

"He was in the hotel room?"

"After you left. He came. He doesn't like you. He wanted to play hide-and-seek again. But I felt better after cleaning up and stuff, and I could ignore him."

Flimsier still. With each answer she gave, he had more questions. But the bones of his diagnosis still stood.

Sophie was looking at the four corners of the ceiling again, as if the voices she heard came from there. Her slim fingers were gripping her bruised knees with force. She seemed to be trying to back into the corner of her chair.

"Sophie, this was tough for you. I'm very proud of you."

She looked at him fleetingly. She was fading fast. He wished he could reach into her brain and hold it still, keep it from getting swallowed in her sickness. Because while Gordon still had his questions about specifics, he felt strongly that Sophie West was schizophrenic. Her condition manifested itself in the form of delusions—hallucinations and voices. As he watched her worsen by degrees, it ripped him to pieces that all he could do was sit in his chair. He refused to show the dismay he felt. He steeled himself.

"We're gonna figure this out, Sophie," he said, trying his

best to keep authority in his voice, even as Sophie let out a soft whine.

As if on cue, Dianne West knocked perfunctorily on the door and then opened it a moment later. She had a blanket that looked worn, most likely a comfort object from Sophie's childhood. She went immediately to her daughter and put it around her, tucking it rather tighter than necessary, almost as if she were willing her daughter to keep herself bottled up and pulled together. Sophie buried her head into her mother's shoulder.

"I think that's all for today," Dianne said, annoyance in her voice. "If she can manage it, we'll be back tomorrow." Dianne pointed at a tattered piece of notebook paper she left on the couch. "Things are... devolving. I found that in her room."

Gordon looked at it dumbly. He couldn't quite make it out. When he turned back to Dianne, she had helped Sophie to stand and was already moving across the room to the door.

Gordon watched from the steps as Dianne looked up and down the street, keeping near the building with an arm around Sophie until her driver arrived. The driver pointedly looked away as he held the back door of the sedan, and Sophie was ushered in as if being chased by paparazzi. They drove away without another word to Gordon.

GORDON PULLED into the parking lot at Waterstones, still distracted by Sophie and her story of Mo. He wasn't in the mood for idle, subtly probing chat with his mother about his social life and new relationship, not even over scotch and a delicious Waterstones Cobb salad. Nor did he want the inevitable Deborah Pope diagnosis when she picked up on his mood, which she always did. His mother was retired, but she was always the first to say that there was no such thing as a retired psychiatrist. She would ask him to talk out his frustrations, which was the problem. He couldn't explain what was nagging him about Sophie's case, other than the fact that she was a schizophrenic that didn't quite fit the mold. But his mother set her watch by those bimonthly lunches. Not attending had far graver consequences for his long-term mental well-being.

His phone rang as he put his car in park. The ID read Mother.

"Hi, Mom," Gordon answered. "Sorry I'm late. I'm just parking, I'll be right in."

"Don't bother, honey," his mother replied. "I'm afraid I'm going to have to cancel lunch."

Gordon nearly dropped the phone into his lap.

"Hate to do it," she said sadly, as if reluctantly turning down that second martini. "It's just that I'm in the hospital."

That time, Gordon did drop the phone. He smacked his head on the steering wheel as he scrabbled for it on the passenger-side floor, and the car horn gave a weak bleat.

His mother was already talking when he corralled it to his ear, but he interjected, "Mother. Mom, can you hear me? Are you hurt? What happened?"

"Oh, I'm at Hopkins in general inpatient. I lost a bit of time. Woke up on the floor of the kitchen. But no, I'm not hurt."

Gordon finally gathered a breath. He steadied himself against the car door, as if his rusty coupe was a boat at sea. His mother was tougher than anyone he knew, save maybe Dana, but she was still seventy-two years old. A fall was a fall. He felt as if he'd dodged a bullet.

"I might be dying, though," she added, almost as an afterthought.

∿

GORDON WALKED into Johns Hopkins Hospital in a daze, his mind tripping over itself. He punched the down button on the elevator when he meant to go up. He got off on the wrong floor. He'd done countless hours of clinical rotations at Johns Hopkins, yet he had to ask two different people where to find general inpatient. He was told Deborah Pope was admitted at the suite level. Naturally. He felt as if he was falling with every step, as if he'd leapt from a building in a dream and just never hit the ground to wake up.

His mother looked fresh as a daisy. She was dressed in silk two-piece pajamas, legs crossed, reading the *New Yorker* on top of a queen-size bed that would look at home at the Inner Harbor Ritz. Classical music played softly. A big double-paned window was opened outward to catch the last of the sunshine. A glass of iced tea sweated on a wooden table at her right. The suite level was pay-to-play, and the pay was steep, but the amenities were excellent.

She looked up at Gordon and smiled, and there he saw just a hint of the fatigue he'd always feared seeing in her—in a woman never before weary. He wanted to hug her, but he'd only ever hugged her in greeting for so long that he felt as though hugging her then would be admitting some sort of defeat. Instead, he sat down awkwardly in a leather chair by an enormous bouquet of flowers.

"Caesar sent me those. Isn't he sweet?"

"The waiter? From Waterstones? Are you serious? He knew about this before I did?"

"Oh, by moments. I called to tell them I'd be canceling

the reservation, one thing led to another, he sent me flowers immediately. Such wonderful service there. Wonderful people."

Gordon flopped his briefcase on the ground and leaned back heavily. The leather puffed out around him.

"What the hell, Mom?" he said, more of a statement than a question.

"It's true. Breast cancer. Stage three. Not good." She folded down her page in the *New Yorker* and turned toward Gordon.

"Are you kidding me?" Gordon took off his glasses and rubbed his eyes. He suddenly felt as though he could fall asleep right there, which he thought was a strange reaction to trauma. Very possum-like.

"Is this why you blacked out?"

"No. I actually found out about it several weeks ago. I was trying to find a way to tell you. I had my first round of radiation therapy earlier this week. Sapped me a bit more than I'd expected."

Gordon could only blink at her. "You've known about this for *weeks*?"

"I was trying to find a way to tell you—"

"How about 'Gordon, I've got cancer.' That would have worked. Three weeks ago."

"Get a hold of yourself. This is a private floor. No hysterics up here." His mother stared sternly at him until he closed his mouth. "We both know you're quite busy these days. Getting the practice up and running again and whatnot—"

"No no no." Gordon waved her off in much the same way she often preempted others. "Don't you dare throw this back on me. This is about you thinking you can go it alone. Not wanting to seem vulnerable."

She looked down her nose at him. "Thank you for the insight, Dr. Pope. You can mail me the bill."

"What are we gonna do?" Gordon asked, feeling very childish, as if all he could do was throw a tantrum. When his father was on the verge of death, after a heart attack at sixty, he'd felt a calm sense of impending loss. No panic. But his father had been distant, more than a bit of a drinker, and unfaithful. His mother was smothering, more than a bit of a drinker, and faithful as the day is long. She didn't deserve to be sitting in a hospital.

"You don't deserve this, Mom," he said helplessly, the words pouring forth.

"Cancer doesn't care what you deserve, sweetheart," she replied, smiling sadly. "And we're going to keep at it," she added, as if pointing out the obvious. "I'm going to radiate the tumor to operable size and then get a double mastectomy."

Gordon choked on his own spittle, coughing loudly. His mother marched on.

"And you're going to keep treating your new patients. What are you working on these days? Your papers spilled out all over the floor."

"A double mastectomy?"

"Yes, honey. It's already scheduled. Now, tell me about work. I like hearing about your work. Now that you have a bit of it. Is that drawing yours? If so, I'd stick to psychiatry." Deborah pointed at the paper-strewn floor, her silver bracelets jingling gently.

Gordon followed her dumbly. She was pointing at Sophie's picture: a family huddled under a black table surrounded by fire—and a grinning boy standing atop, crude, but visible—a childish drawing, most likely done in the depths of one of her psychotic breaks.

"I think it's a bit of a family portrait. A drawing from a new patient I took on," Gordon said. "A very troubled young woman who sets fires that she can't remember starting. Still a girl, really. Just twelve. I'm having a bit of trouble with her diagnosis."

Just talking about something else—anything else—shattered the bubbling panic that crept up Gordon's throat like bad booze. The spinning roulette wheel of his mind settled upon the category of *work*, a well-worn groove, and he found himself able to take his first clear breath since arriving. His mother smiled briefly at him, as if she had known all along just how to bring him around.

"Is she the one grinning like an imp?"

Gordon shook his head. "She's under the table to the right, the blonde with her head down. But the one grinning like an imp set the fire."

"A brother?"

"Her imaginary friend. Mo."

His mother sucked in a breath through her teeth. "A twelve-year-old fire starter who blames her imaginary friend. And here I thought things might get easier for you after the sleepwalkers."

Gordon traced the figures in the drawing lightly with his fingers, and for a moment he forgot he was in a hospital. He might have been across the table from his mother at Waterstones, waiting for a refresh of his cocktail.

"There's more. She's getting external impressions of dread, existential dread that she ties to an impending and unavoidable abduction and assault, maybe a rape. Both of her and her mother. Her imaginary friend tells her the only way to stay safe is to burn."

"You think she's schizophrenic."

"I think so, yes," Gordon said before tilting his head in reconciliation to his own doubts. "Maybe. Maybe not."

Gordon hadn't had a chance to take a good look at the picture yet, in his hurry to get to the hospital. The way Dianne had pointed to it was unsettling, as if she wanted to be gone by the time he looked at it. He found Dianne in the picture, underneath the table, to Sophie's right. She looked just as haunted as Sophie did. The man to Sophie's left was likely her father, Simon. His eyes looked neither sad nor scared, nor wide and manic like Mo's. His were hollow black circles.

"That was three answers, Gordon," Deborah said.

"When I first met her, she was recovering from some sort of episode in a hotel room. Her mother is very protective, both of Sophie and of their family reputation."

Deborah nodded. She understood well about the importance of neighborly reputation. In that, at least, Deborah Pope and Dianne West would find a lot of common ground.

"She was organizing herself out of it using an obsessive-compulsive routine."

"OCD is an indicator of deeper trauma. And a symptom of full-blown psychosis," his mother said.

She'd moved to the side of the bed. If Gordon squinted, he could almost make himself believe that she was across a table adorned with two chilled bowls of Waterstones' Cobb salad.

"It's also a common indicator of extreme anxiety. Not necessarily a full psychotic break," he replied. "I don't feel great about the light benzodiazepine routine I put her on, as it is. But her anxiety is through the roof. I hate diagnosing schizophrenia because..."

"Because once you do, there's no going back."

Gordon nodded. The soft beep of her vitals machines

brought him back to the room. The weight of Sophie's problems, coupled with the reality of his mother's diagnosis, dragged him down in his seat. His world seemed to visibly darken.

"Schizophrenia has no real cure. Only management. It's lifelong. And the medicine is brutal. And she's so young. Schizophrenic breaks don't usually happen to women until their twenties." Gordon rattled each fact off with a flick of his finger.

"You sound like you're making excuses. Like that's what other people might say to you to convince you otherwise. What do *you* feel, Gordon?"

Gordon dropped his head back on the chair, gazing at the ceiling. A particle-board ceiling. A hospital ceiling. All the fancy lighting and queen beds and fresh linens in the world couldn't change that. Couldn't change what his mom was facing. What Sophie was facing.

"It comes back to Mo. The problem is the specificity of him. He's too well-defined of an entity for a schizophrenic. Even one that is delusional. Or hallucinating. The literature describes voices without faces. Orders without origin. Schizophrenics may feel compelled to do things like burn, but I can't think of a case I've come across, or even read about, where a delusional patient so clearly understands the source of the voices."

"Mo."

"Mo." Gordon nodded. "He's a teenage boy. He wears jeans and a dirty T-shirt and pads around shoeless. Sophie can describe the sounds of his feet." Gordon pointed to the picture again. "He has a big Cheshire grin and wears a black ball cap down low over his face. And he tells her that burning everything to the ground is the only way to stay safe in Baltimore."

68 B. B. GRIFFITH

"I know a fair number of people who might agree with little Mo," Deborah said drolly.

"Mother."

"Metaphorically, of course," she added, holding up her hands. "But either way, it sounds like you've got a lot on your plate."

Gordon met her eyes and thought he saw a smile there, a measure of delight in the mountain Gordon had in front of him. And pride. Deborah Pope's own special brand of pride, only given when the whistles blew and her son was faced with the moment when he had to go over the top and charge the hill. He scrunched up his nose a bit to keep the water from his eyes. She looked like someone watching her child wave from the front step of the school before she was forced to turn away from him—maybe for good.

"Mom, I'm gonna stay with you here. I'll sleep in this chair."

"Nonsense. Their care is fabulous here. The chair would only give you back problems."

"Well then, I'll have them wheel in a bed. For whatever you're paying, they can wheel in a bed."

"Gordon—"

"I'm gonna be here, Mom. I'm gonna be with you through all this. Right here."

"Gordon, enough," she said kindly.

Gordon cleared his throat and dropped his head. The lump was painful in his throat.

"Here's what is going to happen. You will live your life. You will treat your patient. You will do what you have to do. And so will I. Now go home and get some rest. You're no good to anybody sleeping in a chair and waiting for your mother to go under."

Gordon coughed. "Mom!"

"The knife, Gordon. Under the knife. My heavens. Don't be so morbid." There, a little more of the old twinkle in her eye.

Gordon felt ashamed that he'd ever thought to skip lunch. What an ass he was. Spoiled. He'd been spoiled. And the other shoe had finally dropped.

His mother seemed to see the swelling of his guilt. Perhaps she felt it in the pregnant pause between them— Gordon had learned everything he knew about listening from his mother. She placed one disturbingly thin hand over Gordon's, stopping whatever confession he'd felt bubbling up.

"Trust me, honey, there will be plenty of time to wallow later in life. Not now. Go."

So Gordon went.

GORDON DROVE AROUND IN A FOG. He hardly registered the liquid sunset that brought the burnished trees to life and set brief fire to the hundreds of office windows lining Monument Street. His mind was awash with worry, for Sophie and for his mother, to the point where he felt as if he was no longer struggling to stay above the churning waters but instead had found some sort of numb stasis within them—not drowning but not really breathing either. He didn't realize where he was going until he was nearly there.

He knocked on Dana's front door, staring blankly at the thatched fall wreath of yellow leaves and red berries hanging in front of his face. Chloe opened the door, with Maria close behind, watching. Chloe gazed up at him through beautiful brown eyes that looked a hair too large for her face. Her mother's eyes. She was dressed in a shiny bubblegum-pink tracksuit. She thrust both her hands in the pockets like an adorable little gangster.

"Hi, Chloe." Gordon tried not to sound as though he'd been on the verge of sobbing most of the afternoon.

"Hi, Gordon," Chloe said.

"That's Dr. Pope, sweetheart," Maria said.

Gordon knew Maria was being polite, but he couldn't help but feel that she also liked the distance of the *Dr. Pope*. Dr. Pope had just started seeing her daughter. *Gordon* was a step along the way to *Gord* or even *Dad*, neither of which either Chloe or her grandmother seemed particularly enthusiastic about right now.

"I like your pink suit," Gordon said.

"Thanks," Chloe said. "I got it from gymnastics."

Gordon was about to ask her more. About gymnastics. About school. About her life. About anything. He thought too hard about where to start, and in the awkward silence, Chloe jumped in.

"Are you looking for Mom? She's at work still. She works all night tonight."

Gordon nodded. He should have called first. He wanted to tell Chloe that he wouldn't mind hanging out with her for a bit. Maybe between them, they could find a way to make it so he didn't feel like such a dope around the family. He'd never been around Maria and Chloe without Dana as a buffer. He wanted to, at some point, but just then, it sounded exhausting. Instead, he nodded and turned to go.

"Will you tell her I stopped by?" Gordon asked, pausing.

"Sure." Chloe nodded vigorously.

"Bye, Chloe," Gordon said. Then he craned to look behind her. "Bye, Maria."

Maria smiled benignly. "Goodbye, Dr. Pope."

In the silence of the car once more, he decided to call Dana. He plucked his phone from his pocket but paused when he saw his voice mail had logged twelve missed calls from a number listed as Unavailable. He had five voice mails. At first, he thought they must be from the hospital earlier, trying to get hold of him to tell him his mother had been admitted. The first message was a quick hang-up, mere seconds. So was the second. Odd, but Hopkins had HIPAA regulations against what could and couldn't be said on an answering machine, so perhaps they were waiting to speak to him personally. The third was similar but slightly longer. He heard a soft intake of breath, as if someone was about to speak, then the click of disconnecting.

Gordon furrowed his brow and pressed Next.

That time, someone was definitely breathing, soft and steady. It went on for ten seconds. By then, a strange feeling of dread was skittering across the back of Gordon's neck although he couldn't say why.

The fifth was the longest yet—twenty seconds of soft, steady breathing, a bit faster than his own. Childlike. As was the voice that spoke in a whisper.

"Leave us alone."

Click.

Gordon took his phone from his ear and stared at it as if he could read more from its blank screen. He played the message over and over again, trying to discern anything from the background during the soft breathing, but he could hear nothing. He had the feeling that whoever was on the other end was thinking hard about whether to speak.

"Leave us alone."

Gordon thought it sounded like a boy. A young boy. However, it could just as easily have been a girl. The voice had yet to fall into either category over the phone. When

Gordon had been in his early teens, he was mistaken for Deborah Pope over the phone more often than not—enough so that he stopped answering, enough so that when his own voice started to crack, that was actually a bit of a relief.

He knew, with a certainty that he had no medical basis for but that was nonetheless undeniable—as sure as the slow shiver that now traced its way down his spine like a single drop of sweat—that the voice belonged to Mo.

Somehow, Mo was talking to him through Sophie. Somehow, she'd gotten his personal number and let Mo take over. His diagnosis was thrown to the wind. If Mo was able to call Gordon, that meant he was enough of a presence within Sophie that he actually existed. He had his own personality.

Perhaps Mo was a separate and distinct personality within Sophie. Perhaps the young girl was suffering from Dissociative Identity Disorder—multiple personalities within one. He'd been given another piece of the puzzle, but again it seemed to have no true home in the overall picture—as if three sides had clicked but the fourth still stuck. Sophie said that she remembered Mo's steps. She heard his voice. She saw him as separate from herself. Those who suffered from multiple-personality disorders often functioned for years without being aware of their separate selves. Many had no idea they were afflicted. Those that were aware of their other selves considered them a part of a whole, as living within. Not Sophie. Sophie saw Mo in front of her. Around her. Outside of her.

Whether Mo was Sophie's delusion or, as was looking more and more likely, a part of Sophie herself, Gordon couldn't say. It seemed like both, which didn't fit cleanly into either. He found he was grinding his teeth. He checked the time on the message. As recently as forty minutes before, Mo had been out in full force, which meant he had to get to Sophie before she hurt herself or others.

His phone buzzed again. At first, he thought it was another voice mail, perhaps from Mo. Anything from the entity himself might serve as a tool he could use to help secure Sophie's mind, to bring her back from mania without delving into the deep end of antipsychotics. If he worked quickly enough, perhaps he could exorcise that delusion and help her to realize a life apart from Mo so she could become her own woman without that shadow hanging over her.

No voice mail that time, only a text message from Dianne, but it confirmed his worst fear. It read, "Sophie has gone missing."

CHAPTER SIX

The smell of old smoke hung in the air, the same way that an unpacked tent can throw an invisible dusting of campfires past into the air. Whoever had turned on the gas and sparked the science lab had set one heck of a fire, but if their aim was to torch the whole school, their job was unfinished. Dana was counting on the fact that, in her experience, arsonists hated unfinished work.

She panned the east wing of the school from where she and Marty sat in the minivan. She saw no movement other than the quiet flutter and twist of a wide swath of police tape that cordoned off the burned area. The moon seemed to have fled the scene as well, casting only intermittent light from a great distance. The only person talking within half a mile was Marty.

"It's roomy. I'll give it that."

"What?" Dana replied absently, eyes straining.

"The ol' family wagon here." Marty thumped the roof with his fist. "You could fit a whole day care in this thing. I thought you only had Chloe."

"When I bought it, I'd planned on more," Dana said

flatly. She was tired, on her second straight night inside Merryville without much to show for it. All she had to go on was a bunch of creepy drawings and a hunch. Meanwhile, her new boyfriend was walking around with his head in the clouds, proving her mother right with every visit. And right then, she didn't feel much like talking.

Marty dropped his hand and softly cleared his throat, nodding and looking away. She felt guilty. Her problems weren't his fault.

"It's all right, Marty. That was then. All that's left of that me is this car."

That had been her line for a long time. Recently, however, she felt less force behind it, which concerned her. Thoughts she'd packed away long before were bubbling up again, like what it meant that she'd never feel the sure swelling of her belly again, and what a good big sister Chloe would make. She shoved those thoughts to the back of her mind. She'd hated being pregnant at the time, found the sensations that came with growing a child more annoying than inspiring or beautiful. She hadn't cared to repeat the process for years and years—thanked God repeatedly, in fact, that she had only Chloe to care for after the divorce. Then she fell for a man that couldn't give her a child, and all of a sudden, her hormones were going haywire. She was forty years old, for God's sake—hardly the time for her body to start waxing nostalgic about pregnancy.

"What I meant to say was not all of us can drive souped-up muscle cars. I gotta strap in more than my gym bag." She put a smile behind the barb that brought Marty around again.

"My baby's not just any muscle car," Marty said, perking back up. "She's a Dodge Charger. Hellcat edition. Stupid fast. Seven hundred horsepower..." He trailed off.

He'd gone full car mode with Dana before and knew it went right over her head. "How's Chloe doin', by the way?" he asked sheepishly.

"She's still a little weirded out by me and Gordon," Dana said truthfully. "She's been singing along to her cartoons louder than usual when he's around."

"What, she doesn't like him?" Marty asked, a gleam in his eye. "I thought he was supposed to be a wizard with kids."

"Yeah, well. He is... with his patients. He's sort of like a fish out of water with Chloe." Dana shook her head. "Or maybe all three of us are flopping around a bit."

Marty leaned back and crossed his thick arms, "You two, maybe. Not Chloe. That girl kicks ass. Maybe he's intimidated."

Dana snorted a laugh. She thought of Chloe in her pink tracksuit, dancing around to her cartoons, her shoes sparkling up a storm. Very intimidating stuff.

Dana gestured out of the windshield with a tic of her head. "How about you just keep an eye out for the kid we should really be afraid of."

Marty tapped the top of the car above the open window as he watched the darkened school. "You really think the kid'll come back?"

Dana nodded slowly. "The far side of the lab was torched, but the side nearest the doors was only singed. Soaking wet paper everywhere, only half burned. He set kindling on both sides, but only the near side caught. Arsonists tend to be perfectionists, no matter what age. At the very least, they might come by again to check it out."

So Marty and Dana settled in and waited.

And waited.

And waited.

. . .

DANA FELT a tapping on her shoulder. She shot up and felt something firmly pressing her back down at the sternum. She almost screamed until she placed herself. Still in her car. Still with Marty, who had his arm barred across her, like a burly mother holding her child back during a hard stop. With his other hand, he pressed a finger to his lips.

Marty pointed out toward the school. After Dana's heart stilled, she could focus long enough to see the dark windows, as gaping and empty as they'd been when she first turned the car off to sit and watch. She shook her head, unable to see anybody.

"By the big tree," he whispered.

The cicadas had long gone to sleep, their roar replaced by the soft chirp of crickets. She looked at the clock and flushed with embarrassment. Marty had let her sleep until nearly three in the morning. She frowned at him, but he pointed again.

Dana watched the big tree they'd walked under with the janitor the day before, an enormous white oak that silently dropped leaves at a steady rate. All she saw was its dark mass, weakly lit in passing by the cloud-covered moon.

Then her eyes caught something, not much more than a flickering of shadow but visible in the harsh relief between the tree and the lighter fields beyond. She held her breath. The flickering pulled back behind the tree until she'd nearly convinced herself it was a trick of her imagination. Then a figure emerged, one limb at a time. Slowly. Like a shadow peeling itself from the wall until she could see its outline clearly in the space between.

He was small and thin, definitely child sized, possibly adolescent. He stood with his hands on his hips like a skinny superhero surveying his domain. No cape, but he did have a hat, a baseball cap, brim slightly to the side.

"That's our guy," Dana whispered. She felt it was a him. Something in the challenge of the stance said *boy* to her. He looked like a boy out on a dare. She could almost see his grin.

For a moment, she thought he was looking at them. They were at least a hundred feet away from the tree, one of several cars parked on the street outside the school, including the busted Land Rover—so she doubted he'd seen them. Still, the featureless outline of his shadow gave the illusion that he was staring at them in silence. Even the crickets had paused.

After several frozen moments, all three of them stock still, he clearly stepped away from them until he was lost in the shadows of the building at the cordon. The tape fluttered then went still again.

Both Dana and Marty slowly opened their doors, stepped out, then shut them with the barest push and click. They crossed the street like thieves. Dana felt strongly that direct confrontation would go badly for them. The boy's movements had been sure, quick. She could picture him bolting and disappearing into the night, their chance missed. Marty seemed to know that as well. He was good. And she owed him, no matter what came of this night. She was the one driving the stakeout, having told him to give up his Saturday night to sit there. She knew he looked up to her. Dana made a mental note to get more sleep. Senior officers did not fall asleep on watch. It was unlike her.

No matter how tired she had been, she was wide awake the second she stepped out of the car. Dana keyed in to every sound, every movement. Ahead of her, the desks had been taken out and arranged in rows under the broken moonlight and the reaching canopy of the massive white oak, each dusted lightly with fallen leaves. More leaves fell upon the detectives as they walked underneath, each floating down in silence, one after the other like lemmings at a cliff.

Dana thought she'd seen the boy go under the cordon, but she wasn't sure. Under the filtered moonlight and amplified silence, everything seemed so dreamlike. She was starting to second guess that she'd ever seen the boy at all. She turned to Marty and shook her head, but then her nose flared with a smell, an acrid, unmistakable scent that drew her in and repelled her at the same time. Gasoline. She nosed about, but the scent left her with a puff of the night breeze.

Marty pointed to his ear. She heard it, too—a whisper like the soft roiling of water in a pot.

Glugluglug.

It was coming from inside the burned-out lab.

Gluglugluglug

Dana dropped all attempts at silence. She took off running, rounding the desks at top speed with Marty beside her. With each step, the smell of gasoline grew stronger until she felt permeated by it. Then she saw him, a single figure standing like a sprinter on the blocks less than fifty feet from her on the edge of the grass outside the broken doors. He had on a black hat, which shadowed his face almost entirely—only his bright-white teeth shone in the night. He wore baggy jeans and a loose T-shirt that hung past his rear. His legs seemed bony and his shoeless feet oversized. He let out a brief, bubbly giggle before covering his mouth. Then he struck a match.

"Race me," he whispered harshly.

Dana could only wave her hands, as if she could blow

out the match from a distance. She didn't even have time to utter a cry as he dropped it on the trampled grass and took off at a tear toward the black maw of the burned-out lab.

The world seemed to freeze. The police tape that surrounded them no longer fluttered. The weak wind died. Dana froze in shock, her hands out. Marty was caught with his mouth open. Only the strange boy seemed able to move, the strange boy and the line of fire that followed him—the boy with a giggle, the fire with a low hiss.

When time snapped back to her, Dana ran after him, not even thinking. She ran as if compelled, as if the fire were pulling her along with a crooked finger of flame. The boy was fast, and he had a head start. Already, he was jumping the larger debris before the outer wall. Dana vaulted it seconds later, but by then, he'd shot through the broken doors, feet slapping the charred linoleum inside, and in an instant, he was swallowed in darkness as surely as if he'd dropped down a hole in the earth. The hole was so black it caught Dana up for a moment, much like a driver instinctively slows before a tunnel. An ancient, ingrained response was telling her *Do not enter that cave. You don't know what is back there.*

Marty was yelling something: *Dana* or perhaps *Don't*. She heard his heavy steps slamming behind her. And she almost did stop, until the snake of fire shot inside the cave ahead of her, and its light, no brighter than a hurricane candle, was still enough to show the glittering teeth of the child just below the brim of his hat, head turned, midstride, eyes aimed at her.

Dana shot along the burn line, chasing the flame. She could smell charred plastic and ash and wet wood. She seemed to dive through each scent, one after the other.

Ahead of her, the boy careened around the aftermath of

the fire as if it was his own bedroom, ducking the bolted tables with ease as they appeared. He was swallowed in darkness in a matter of moments, and at the same time Dana broke through into a new, overwhelming smell of straight gasoline. Then she really did stop. She held up her hands as if she could part the heavy curtain of fumes that watered her eyes and caught her breath in her throat.

Marty started screaming for her.

Dana blinked her eyes against the fumes. She saw the fire crawl forward through a watery haze in the air, and it seemed to her like a burning comet in the darkness of the room,

hurtling with massive speed at the same time as it crawled along across the horizon. Soon, she saw what Marty was screaming about. A spilled canister of gasoline was illuminated by degrees. Then another next to it. And another. And the comet was on a collision course—too far for her to stop it, too close for her to run.

She felt the explosion before she saw it, like the first step into a sauna. A heavy, powerful heat pushed at her with an open palm to the chest. A bloom of fire followed, and it seemed to Dana that the bloom passed through every color of the rainbow before ending in an all-engulfing white. She heard the explosion last of all—a basso thud that felt as if it thrust upward from the ground into the base of her lungs as she was yanked from her feet and out of consciousness.

CHAPTER SEVEN

Gordon creaked to a stop outside the iron-and-ivy gate of the Merryville neighborhood in his whining coupe. He frowned, checking the address Dianne had given him. Everything matched, but he wasn't expecting to be stopped at the gates. He'd known Dianne was wealthy, but Merryville looked like its own little fiefdom, outside and above the world around it.

His brakes roused the attendant from his novel. The man straightened his jacket and stepped from the booth with his clipboard.

"Can I help you, sir?"

"Is Long Lane down this way?" Gordon asked.

"It is. Are you Doctor Pope?"

"I am."

"May I see some identification?"

He looked at Gordon's license over the rims of his spectacles and jotted down its number on his pad, checking his watch to note the time. Gordon glanced at the clock. If one in the morning was an unusual time for visitors, the attendant didn't let on.

He handed back the license, nodded, and said, "Number eight Long Lane. Straight ahead."

The gate swung open noiselessly. The road ahead was dark and lined with trees like ancient sentinels. Gordon was uncomfortably aware of the slap and whine of his fraying engine belt as he drove forward.

Number eight Long Lane would have taken up one through eight in any city neighborhood. He'd never seen an estate so large that close to Baltimore proper. It looked like something more suited to Bethesda, where Gordon had grown up and the lots had rounded driveways and the occasional horseback rider could be seen cantering through the faraway fields.

The house itself consisted of three parts: a center structure of white stone and columned wood and two redbrick wings, each with a glittering slate roof lit at intervals from the ground. Every window was flanked by whitewashed shutters, every edge sharp, every tree trimmed for full fall effect. The lights were on inside, illuminating the windows at intervals throughout, but Gordon saw no movement behind them.

Gordon squeaked to a stop and parked on the street. He took the long walk over heavy flagstone to the front door, where he cleared his throat and rang the doorbell. A brass chime rang through the entire house like an echo in a canyon.

Then silence.

Gordon frowned. He tried knocking on the heavy door but felt as if his rapping barely penetrated the wood. He rang the doorbell again.

Silence.

Gordon pulled out his phone and tried the number from which Dianne had texted him. It rang. And rang. And rang.

Gordon dropped his hands to his side. He let out a slow, steady breath. The ringing continued. He cocked his head, listening. The sound jumped from his phone through the door and inside the house. Dianne's phone, at least, was nearby.

"Dianne?" Gordon stepped forward and placed one hand on the door, the other on the knob. "Dianne, are you there? It's Gordon."

It can't possibly be open. Not after the gate and the guard and the clipboard and signing in...

The front door opened at a turn of the brass knob. It swung in as if on oiled bearings. The house smelled orange-scented clean. It was lit in the manner that an empty hotel corridor is lit—at intervals and by lights that Gordon doubted ever turned off.

"Hello? If anyone is here, I'm coming in." *Please don't sic the hounds on me.*

He flicked his phone out again and redialed. He listened, eyes wide. He almost jumped back out onto the porch when Dianne's phone buzzed to life straight ahead of him. As it rang, it spun slowly like an angry, wounded wasp on the floor, dead ahead. He walked forward, through the gleaming marble foyer and into an expansive great room of dark wood, the nexus of the house. A dimmed chandelier hung above him, drawing his eye up the staircase ahead and along the balustrades of three floors of rooms. Pastoral artwork hung on the walls in burnished wood frames. A lacquered black grand piano sat near one corner, top open, ready for play. Dianne's phone buzzed at the base of a brass sculpture of an angry-looking buffalo standing just to the left of the stairway. Afraid to pick it up, he stared at it until it quieted.

He looked up the stairs and grimaced, his hands on his hips. Going up there seemed somehow more of an invasion, as if there were degrees of penetration. In the great room, with the foyer just behind and the door still open, he was barely in the house. He could still bolt. But up there? Up there, he was in it.

Gordon's eye was drawn toward movement from behind the stairs, toward the back of the main level. A white lace curtain fluttered out like a woman's dress in the sparse wind coming through wide-open double doors leading to the back patio and darkened lawn beyond.

Gordon walked toward the open doors. That he could pass right through, in and out, as if he had never been there, gave him some small measure of comfort. He pawed down the billowing curtain and pushed it behind heavy purple drapes nearby before stepping out.

Two floodlights slammed on, and Gordon threw his arms in front of his eyes. He stood still, hands up, until his hammering heart subsided. He waited for the shouts and accusations, but as his breathing steadied, the lights shut off again. *Motion sensors. Of course.*

"Dianne?" he called into the blind darkness. "Sophie?"

The last locusts of the season clicked softly in half-hearted response, their sleep disturbed. The crickets quieted.

As his eyes adjusted, Gordon saw in the near distance a small shed by a fledgling tree, which looked out of place surrounded by such grand compatriots. A new tree. He recalled the story of the fire. Dianne had said Sophie had started it in a tree house and it spread to one wing of the house. Gordon couldn't see any damage to the house from where he stood, but the fire had been years before, and houses like that one were quickly and spotlessly repaired.

Old-growth trees, on the other hand, were not so easily replaced.

Gordon walked across the lawn, shading his eyes as the lights clicked on again at his movement. He saw that the shed was more like a small house, a beautiful little wooden playhouse complete with little windows and little shutters and a little hanging basket with live flowers. The door said Sophie's Place in painted white stencil on a miniature mailbox outside a small door that looked remarkably similar to the front door of the house proper. That, too, was open.

Gordon crossed from grass to a fresh cedar-chip flooring, and he felt confident he was standing where a large white oak tree had once stood before its charred remains were ground from the earth and Sophie's Place built anew. *The next best thing to a tree house if you no longer have the tree.*

Gordon pushed the little door open farther. It cut a track through a layer of dust on the floor of the single room inside. The floodlights shut off, and he was plunged into darkness. He pulled out his phone and used it to light what he could, which was almost everything. Glittering flecks of dust floated slowly in the air, nearly still. He guessed Dianne and Simon had had it rebuilt immediately after the fire two years back, perhaps thinking their troubled child still needed a place of her own. Perhaps she'd sat a handful of times in those small chairs, shoved to the far wall and stacked atop a small table like a little shuttered restaurant. No longer. The place felt forgotten, which made the footprints Gordon saw all the more out of place.

The small divot of the ball of a foot and five little tufts of toes, like instructions for a child's dance routine, repeated itself along the perimeter of the room. After years of neglect, someone had recently been in there—tiptoed or pranced on bare feet.

Gordon recalled Sophie's feet sticking out from the corner of the bed, her shoes neatly placed one way, then another, then back again after each of her washings. He knew the girl didn't like to wear shoes in the depths of her attacks.

Gordon followed the prints with his light, and they took him on a mad waltz around the little playhouse. The trail ended at a neat row of colored pencils, organized in shades in their open box, placed flush against the corner opposite the door. They spanned the color wheel from black to white, each the same sharpness, each the same height, which made the single missing color as obvious as a gap tooth. The pencils skipped from yellow to red. No orange among them.

Gordon heard a soft thump in the distance, and he flinched down. The sound unsettled him in a primal way, like a car wreck or a muffled scream. His gut told him he'd just heard an explosion and it was nearby.

Standing in that playhouse marked by a sick young girl who in all likelihood was very recently not in her right mind —who was likely following the voices in her head—in that moment, surrounded by floating specks of the past and ill portents of the present, Gordon knew that the explosion he'd heard was because of Sophie.

He rushed from the playhouse, and the lights snapped on again. He spun in a circle, looking for anything that might tell him where that awful *whump* had come from, but the lights were too bright and the trees too tall. The sky was nothing but a patch of black seen straight up from the bottom of a well.

He started toward the back doors again, planning to

follow the sound out front, in his car if need be. It couldn't have been that far away, a quarter mile at most—not that Gordon had heard all that many explosions in his life. He tried to think of what the fireworks shows at the Bethesda Country Club had sounded like from Windmill Hill, where he'd sat as a child. That had been about a quarter mile—

Someone was in the house.

Gordon dropped to the ground and froze. He'd caught only a glimpse, but in that second, he'd seen a man in the house. Tall and broad. Gordon flattened himself in the vast expanse of the floodlit lawn like a petrified rabbit and tried not to panic. Anybody who even glanced outside would see him plain as day.

So he started rolling. He rolled like a log, over and over himself, staining his khakis while his brand-new shirt, one of two, came untucked and billowed around him like a sheet until he hit the metal edging of the perimeter. He smelled cedar and, underneath it, the barest scent of burned wood. At first, he had the absurd thought that he'd somehow run into the burned wing of the house, but that was long covered over. He smelled new burn on the weak wind, although in a way, the new burn was just a continuation of the old. Another entry in a long story of fire that seemed dedicated to this place.

All Gordon could do was lie still, dug in against the wood chips, as the man walked around slowly inside the house. He could hear his footsteps pick up then pause. The man was looking for something. Or someone.

"Sophie?" he said, gruff and demanding. An order.

The sweat Gordon had worked up in the rolling and the hiding froze on his brow as surely as if he'd walked into an icebox. He recognized that voice.

"Dianne? Are you here?"

The way he spoke their names sounded as though he was familiar with them, but his tone was harsh and clipped, annoyed. An underlying vein of anger was barely concealed. He stepped to the open back door and paused before stepping fully outside, where Gordon could see him. Warren Duke pondered the floodlights then turned his gaze to the playhouse. Gordon didn't dare breathe. The lieutenant, now major, had never liked Gordon. To say the least. *Hated* Gordon was much more accurate. Gordon had his theories—maybe because he refused to be pushed around by the man, maybe because he was a "civvie" inserting himself in police matters, maybe because he'd created quite a bit of paperwork for Duke's district recently —but in the end, he had no real answer. Perhaps Duke simply didn't like the look of Gordon's face.

Whatever the reason, if Duke spotted him, it would end badly for Gordon. Jailed for breaking and entering at best. He'd tried to arrest Gordon before. That Gordon wasn't in jail right then was due purely to the good press he'd given Duke when he broke the sleepwalker case. But good press was fleeting, and there Duke was, somehow, improbably walking out of the back doors of the house of yet another of Gordon's patients as if he owned the place. He was in his official uniform, his preppy jacket and pink oxford gone in favor of the dress blues of the BPD that showed his new rank in the bars on his collar and the bars on his arms. He held his cap in the crook of an elbow with one hand and shaded his eyes with the other. His signet ring flashed brilliant gold in the floodlights. He looked as if he was born into the rank, which Gordon knew wasn't far from the truth. The Duke family ran a textile empire out of the docks—had for generations. Other blue-blood east coasters were born with silver spoons in their mouths. Duke had the whole silver knife set. He was the type of man who could ruin you in Baltimore with a single word to his people, and that was *before* he'd become a major.

He was perhaps twenty feet from Gordon. Close enough to see the pulsing vein in his tanned temple. Gordon was sure he'd be able to smell the man's cologne if the growing smoke smell hadn't been so strong. If Duke made a half turn to his right and took a second to peer into the dark circle just outside the lights, he'd see Gordon sprawled out like a drunk on the lawn. Gordon's panic was real, but it was secondary. His mind was too busy tumbling over itself, trying to piece together what, exactly, Warren Duke was doing there.

He couldn't have followed Gordon. The two of them had stayed as far apart as possible for a month. More accurately, Gordon tried to stay as far from Duke as possible, which wasn't a problem. They didn't exactly run in the same circles. Maybe Duke was simply responding to the explosion. *But why stop by 8 Long Lane first?*

Perhaps he knew about Sophie and Mo and the Merryville fire. Perhaps he'd put everything together.

As Duke panned the backyard, Gordon realized he'd have the unfortunate chance to ask the man himself, in another couple seconds—right before the cuffs went on, most likely.

But then Duke froze, and a heartbeat later, Gordon heard why.

Sirens. Several of them, coming their way. Sirens at night in a neighborhood like that meant something had gone terribly wrong—the explosion really was as bad as Gordon feared. Duke turned around and looked through the house, back out front. Gordon heard the passing of two blaring police cruisers followed by the low whine of a fire truck and the telltale two-tone of an ambulance.

Duke pulled out his phone, glanced at the screen, shook his head, and tucked it back into his breast pocket, muttering a curse. He turned around and walked inside again, closing the glass doors behind him with a locking click.

Gordon lay still, his mind reeling. Only when the lights shut off again, when he was plunged into darkness like a cold pool, did he come to his senses. The bizarre voice mail, the strange house, the explosion, Duke's appearance—he needed to think things through. With Dana. And scotch. Lots of scotch.

He inched his way deeper into the hedges at the edge of the property until he was behind enough shrubbery to stand unnoticed. Then he worked his way to the perimeter of the lawn. The iron gate there was more ornamental than functional, just about shoulder height. He grabbed hold of the blunted top and, after a solid five minutes of scrabbling and huffing, positioned himself to fall down on the far side, directly on the car keys in his hip pocket. He sucked air through his teeth, pushed himself standing, and rubbed his hip vigorously as he looked to see where he was—in a small greenbelt between properties. The street was to his right. He walked until he saw flashes of blue and red dancing off the leaves and vines all around him.

The lights came from his left, around the corner. With his back to the iron gate, he peered around, staying out of view.

He needn't have bothered. Gordon counted three police cars, one fire truck, and one ambulance, but all attention was being paid to the ruined front face of what looked to Gordon like a fancy school. Great gouts of smoke billowed out and up from flashes of lashing flame. But that wasn't what held his focus.

Gordon squinted to better see the work of the medics. Two were kneeling on the ground to either side of someone, and Gordon realized he was fully expecting to find Sophie between them. He prayed he wasn't too late and pushed off the gate. As he walked slowly toward them, his mind raced with how he might explain himself, especially to Warren Duke, who stood as stark and sharp as a marble sculpture by the side of the ambulance, watching as the medics worked.

When he saw Marty Cicero, he thought he was hallucinating. Marty should be off with Dana, at work. Not leaning heavily against the ambulance as if it was the only thing holding him up. Duke held an air of detachment, but Marty seemed tethered to the victim with an almost visible line of emotion, so strong it nearly pitched him over.

One of the medics moved. Gordon saw a gloved hand glistening with blood. Everything slowed for him in that instant, and he saw Dana very clearly—first her ink-dark hair and a sliver of her face, eyes closed, tipped gently to one side. Her mouth was slightly open, as if she was doing nothing more than napping. After only an instant, the medic shifted again and hid her from view, but Gordon knew he would remember that moment as clearly as if it was painted on the back of his eyes.

He ran. Warren Duke turned toward him, and some small part of Gordon's mind registered the look he gave—a look that said he knew he'd be there, knew he had likely been at the house on Long Lane, too. A cold fury fell over Duke that hardened with each step Gordon took, but Gordon didn't care. He pushed past everything and everyone until Marty had to collar him and pull him away, but he couldn't stop Gordon from calling Dana's name again and again and again like a lost child at the supermarket, louder and louder until the medics closed the doors of the ambulance and rocketed away from the broken and billowing schoolhouse, and even then, he still called for her, but the blaring siren drowned out his cries.

CHAPTER EIGHT

M arty's Charger ripped down Highway 83, drafting
just behind the ambulance. The engine of
Gordon's coupe was screaming just to keep him in sight.
Gordon rarely pushed his car past sixty-five. He had little
cause to. Most of his life played out within the city limits.
Normally, he would be terrified the entire car was going to
fall apart around him, but just then he was grateful for the
white-knuckle distraction. It kept him from thinking about
what was happening in the back of that ambulance, from
thinking constantly about that bloody glove and about the
way her mouth had been slightly open.

Hopkins was churning, even at that late hour. The
hospital never slept. Gordon left his car running in the
roundabout. If they needed to move it, they would. Or
they'd tow it. He hardly cared. He met Marty as he was
flashing his badge at the emergency admit desk. Gordon
drafted behind him again into the guts of Hopkins emergency care.

Gordon was hit with déjà vu. It felt to him as if an eternity had passed since he'd been there, but in reality, he'd taken those elevators hours before. The two most important women—most important people—in his life were both at Johns Hopkins Hospital. That his mother and his girlfriend would be admitted within a day of each other struck him as particularly cruel, as evidence of some greater mechanism out to destroy everything good he'd scraped from the barrel of his life.

Both Marty and Gordon were stopped at the door to the surgical floor. Marty spoke with the receptionist at the front desk briefly, his voice remarkably calm when Gordon wouldn't have trusted himself at a whisper. They were told she had gone straight to surgery. The receptionist at the front desk gave them each a color-coded card with a number on it that had been assigned to Dana. They were told to watch the monitors in the waiting room. Dana's number would cycle through from surgery to post op to recovery when visitors were allowed. Purple to green. No reds, of course—nothing that might indicate *how* things were going. Only neutrals.

At some point during Gordon's slow, shell-shocked pacing of the waiting room and hallway beyond, he realized he was alone, and he remembered Marty telling him he was returning to the scene to file a report. He checked the clock and saw he'd been there for nearly two hours and Dana's number was still firmly purple. The frightened hush of the waiting room grated on him, as if the air itself was pulled tight, near to breaking.

Gordon stepped out to the hallway and found himself at the elevators. He glanced at the time again—nearly five in the morning. His mother was an early riser, but she was recovering from her final radiation treatment before she went purple herself, and God knew she had enough on her plate as it was.

Still, he'd never wanted to drop in on his mom so much in his life. It took all he had to pull his hand away from the call button and turn from the elevator doors. What would he say to her anyway? *"Dana's hurt, and it was my patient that hurt her."* Marty had said they were chasing someone. A kid. In a black hat and jeans. Shoeless. They couldn't make a positive ID before the explosion, but it all lined up. Sophie was gone, and Mo had come out. The evidence that the two were one and the same was overwhelming. Yet Gordon's diagnosis still scratched at him like a sharp pebble in his shoe. He could practically hear his mother in his mind. *"You can't force yourself to believe your own diagnosis, Gordon. It's either right or it's wrong."*

True, but you *could* look the facts in the face. And the facts were that his girlfriend was quite possibly on the brink of death, and he was almost positive he knew who'd brought her there.

"Almost positive? Almost isn't a lot to hang a little girl's life on."

He looked up at the nearest monitor for what felt like the thousandth time. Still purple. The woman he loved—for he was sure of that now, he did love her, a pain that acute at the threat of losing her could stem only from love—had been turned into a purple number on a screen.

He was set to meet Sophie in five short hours for their scheduled therapy session. He stood up and took a deep breath. He could do nothing more for Dana in the waiting room. They would call him if her status changed. He fingered the card Marty had given him before leaving.

Marty Cicero
Detective, Baltimore Police Department
Child Protective Investigations

His number was blazoned on the bottom.

Gordon decided he would go home. He would prepare to meet Sophie. And if things went the way he thought they would, he'd be calling the police and placing her in rehabilitative care whether Dianne liked it or not. He didn't feel good about it. He felt as if he was forcing the puzzle, but only because Sophie had forced his hand. He knew Dana might tell him to step back, think rationally, but Dana was a purple number on a screen now, and Gordon's heart was breaking. He had to do *something*.

By the time of Sophie's appointment, Gordon had been notified that Dana was out of surgery. Marty relayed the details with clinical detachment that Gordon instantly recognized as the big man's way of coping with the terrible: second-degree burns on her arms and face and third-degree burns on her hands. The real kicker, the boot to the gut, was that a piece of metal, most likely from one of the canisters of gasoline, had struck her just above the temple. They'd worked for two hours to extract it. Her brain had swelled dangerously. She was in an induced coma until the swelling receded. They didn't know how long that would take—anywhere from one day to one week. Or never.

Gordon needed a hefty swig of scotch before he was able to stop himself from shaking enough to answer the door when Sophie and Dianne rang. He stood, smoothed his blazer and eased his jaw, then opened the door. The afternoon rains that often bookended Baltimore days during fall had just started, and Gordon expected to find daughter and mother in huddled disarray—Sophie unable to meet his eyes, her fingernails black with soot, and Dianne frantic, her perfectly bobbed hair at odd angles.

Instead, he found the two of them as he always had—Dianne eager to begin and to get out of the street, and Sophie with a rumpled look of exhaustion edged with panic. Her backpack was still on, her back bowed, her hands chapped. Gordon couldn't help but look at her nails as she gripped the straps of her pack. No soot to be found.

"Hello, Sophie," Gordon said with effort. "Dianne."

"Hi, Dr. Pope," Sophie said softly before moving aside and past him, toward the back room where their chairs sat. Gordon waited at the door another moment, facing Dianne and waiting for her to speak, to explain why she hadn't been where her phone was when he'd answered her call for help. But she looked at him questioningly.

"What happened last night, Dianne?" he whispered, unable to keep the edge of anger from his voice.

"What do you mean?"

"The text? The *fire*?" Gordon strained to keep his voice low. He had always suspected Dianne was a neglectful parent, but he didn't want to overplay his hand before Sophie could explain herself.

Dianne shook her head slowly. "I was at my writer's group all night. I never texted anyone."

Gordon's head swam. He felt like slamming the door in her face and going to bed. He pulled his phone from his pocket.

"I received several strange voice mails last night from a blocked number. And one text from you. 'Sophie has gone missing.'"

Dianne looked at the text Gordon showed her, but she didn't seem to register his words. She felt her pockets but came up short. She dug in her purse to no avail. Dianne opened and closed her mouth several times. He could see the wheels of her mind working, spinning furiously.

"You don't have your phone, do you?" Gordon asked. He pictured it where he'd left it, on the floor by the statue. He thought about telling her but stopped himself when he felt he wouldn't be able to answer the questions that followed, questions like "What were you doing in my house, and why did you waltz on in when I didn't answer the doorbell?"

"Somebody must have stolen it. But nobody knows you're treating Sophie. Unless..."

"Unless it was Sophie," Gordon said.

Dianne worked her mouth in silence. Gordon thought about dropping another bomb on her while her mind raced to catch up. He knew of at least one other person that seemed familiar with what was happening on Long Lane: Warren Duke. But if Duke was involved and Dianne knew it, that meant she was purposely hiding it from Gordon for some reason. She was crafty and would deflect if asked directly, but perhaps Sophie could provide answers. He checked his watch. Time to get on with the session. He invited Dianne in and helped her to her seat with a glass of water. He left her to her own thoughts as he went to Sophie, closing the door between the rooms.

He could feel the weight of Sophie's eyes with his back still turned. He felt tired, as if his shoes adhered to the floor with every step, just enough that it took an effort to move, just enough to make him weary, as if he was wading through sand. He forced himself to straighten, but that took effort. It occurred to him that he hadn't slept in over twenty-four hours. He was wallowing again. Wallowing did nothing. He'd wallowed for five years before he met Dana. He'd already wallowed once today, and he wasn't about to start again.

He'd meant to move right into things, to greet Sophie as he sat down, hands on his knees, leaning slightly forward and saying, *"So, how have you been?"* the same as every other session. Then he would sit quietly and wait until she felt uncomfortable enough to explain herself, press only where he needed to, and call Marty when he had to.

When he turned to her, he couldn't find the girl he wanted to hand over to the police, the one who delighted in fire. What he found was a girl meticulously plucking at her colored pencils, setting them just so in their case, turning them one at a time so the embossed lettering was out, carefully closing the box, then opening it and doing it again. Her hands were raw, but not from any burns that Gordon could see. They were raw from washing, chapped and cracked, her cuticles bitten to the quick. Little red dots of blood framed each stripped nail. She looked down intently, focusing on her organizing. He noticed that she seemed hung up on one pencil that seemed shorter than the others —the orange one. It was back.

"How are you feeling, Sophie?" he asked. He'd been worried about sounding angry, but instead he was worried about sounding sad, as if he was grieving. That he'd been within a hairbreadth of arresting this girl shamed him. As if taking her away would somehow bring Dana back. That was not the Gordon Pope Dana would be proud of.

"Bad," she said softly. She scratched at her chapped hands and winced. She rubbed her tired eyes with her forearm. She looked like she didn't want to contaminate herself with different parts of herself.

"You've been doing a lot of washing," Gordon said carefully.

Sophie nodded, embarrassed. "I'm trying to remember what happened. It helps me remember what happened."

"What happened when?"

"Last night. And other times too. When I forget things."

"You don't remember what happened last night?" Gordon asked, keeping his voice steady.

Sophie shook her head. "I try to sleep, but I can't because I hear the voices. Then they get so bad that I forget everything. I wake up different places. The back lawn. The library. Downstairs. But I don't think I ever really sleep."

"Does Mo talk to you?"

Sophie nodded. She picked up her colored pencils again and began to pluck each in order, sliding it up a half inch, inspecting the point, resting it down and turning the embossed side out again.

"So Mo talked to you last night, then you can't remember what you did?"

Sophie nodded, plucking, setting, turning. Gordon noticed a small tremor in her hands. He realized she was afraid. She wasn't a girl who delighted in fire. She was a girl who wanted to feel safe, a girl who was doing what she could to feel safe the only way she knew how. By purifying. By scrubbing and by burning. When Sophie couldn't do the burning, Mo did it for her.

"Have you been taking your medicine?" Gordon asked.

Sophie nodded again. "Mom makes me take the pills every morning."

The benzodiazepine should have built up a solid base in her system by then, but she seemed as anxious as ever—more so, even. He'd hesitated to prescribe full-blown antipsychotics—the side effects were often severe and long lasting, and they included things like breast cancer and blindness and were especially potent for adolescents—but his hesitation might have very well cost Dana her life. He wouldn't make the same mistake twice.

He pulled out his prescription pad and tapped his pen on it. He recognized the power of drugs, but he always had an aversion to medicating a symptom into submission as a first line of defense. It felt like giving up. If only the damn puzzle pieces fit together better...

"Sophie, do you remember calling me last night?"

Sophie paused in her ordering and bit her lip. Gordon could see she was trying, really trying. Her eyes wetted lightly with tears of frustration from how hard she was trying to remember, but she shook her head.

"What about sending a text? Do you remember sending me a text from your mom's phone?"

Gordon showed her his phone: "Sophie has gone missing," but Sophie shook her head, her eyes rimmed with red. She sorted faster, faster, until one of the pencils caught and tumbled the entire box from her hands. The box struck the floor and threw its contents all over the rug, and for a moment both Gordon and Sophie froze. Sophie's shaking hands moved slowly to her mouth.

"It's okay, Sophie," Gordon said, holding his own hands out to her as if he could dampen her panic. "It's okay. We can gather them up again. Look." He moved toward the pile until she started crying softly—a sound so desperately sad and broken that Gordon imagined it was similar to the sound dogs made in strange kennels in the dead of night. He sat back down without another word.

Dianne shot into the room with her hands out as if prepared to tackle someone. She saw Sophie and Gordon, and her eyes measured the distance between them.

"She dropped her pencils," he said calmly but clearly, yet his voice was overrun by Sophie's one long wail. Dianne moved over to Sophie and grasped her shoulder, shaking it. "Sophie, this is your mother. Get a hold of yourself this instant."

Sophie didn't even seem to register Dianne. She slid to the floor and began to gather her pencils furiously, holding out the hem of her plaid skirt and piling them on as if the floor were poison to them, and to a child with severe OCD, it likely was. The pencils were contaminated now. She would have to clean them in her own way. But that would take time, and from the way Sophie's eyes rolled continuously to the four corners of the ceiling, he knew they didn't have time. The voices were beginning to call to her. Mo was beginning to call to her.

Still, Dianne shook her, calling her name over and over again and shushing her.

"Dianne, you have to let her gather them herself," Gordon said.

Dianne didn't seem to hear him. She looked close to a panic attack herself. He wouldn't touch Sophie—that broke protocol, especially considering her condition—but he could remove Dianne. In one swoop, his grabbed her by the shoulders, stood her upright, then stepped between them.

"Dianne," he said flatly. "Enough. Let her go through her own motions. It's the only way she'll calm down."

Dianne breathed heavily through her nose and held a balled fist to her front teeth. She looked furious and dismayed at the same time. Her eyes flitted to the window Gordon had opened earlier to hear the rain. She was worried about sound carrying out to the street, worried about her daughter causing a scene again. She couldn't catch a deep breath. She seemed embarrassed and a bit ashamed, both of Sophie and of herself.

As Sophie gathered all her pencils onto her dress, she calmed from a cry to a mewl then a whimper, but her eyes still panned the ceiling above. Dianne watched her daughter with wringing hands, her head tilted forward as if she wanted to rest it on Sophie's shoulder. Gordon dropped his hands to his sides and rolled his neck, his exhaustion redoubled. He'd gone from blood boiling to cold weariness too many times already that day. He felt raw and frayed, as if he'd been turned inside out.

"Dianne, it's my professional opinion that your daughter is in the middle of a psychotic break. If she isn't hospitalized soon, she may spiral downward, and she may hurt herself... or others. If she hasn't already," Gordon added, regretting it immediately when Dianne's eyes flicked to his in a heartbeat.

Gordon went no further, but he knew Dianne had caught his meaning, and he knew from her silence that she understood. Dianne was a strange and distant woman, but she wasn't stupid. She'd dodged his question about the fire at Merryville Prep earlier, but that didn't mean she was ignorant of it. She could put two and two together.

Then she shook her head.

"Absolutely not. She needs to recuperate at home until this passes, just like it did last time."

"When she nearly burned down the house, you mean," Gordon said quietly, gesturing Dianne aside as he spoke. He watched Sophie carefully, unsure of what he should and shouldn't tell her directly at that time, unsure of what she would understand even if he did.

Dianne crossed her arms in front of her small frame and pierced Gordon with the flat, off-center gaze of a dug-in mule. "Houses can be repaired, trees replanted. Those are just things. We're talking about her life, here. Her reputation. This will pass just like it did last time." On the ground behind them, Sophie began meticulously placing her pencils in the box, at an angle, as if constructing a ship in a bottle. Her crying had stopped entirely, but her eyes still raced across the ceiling, and now and then she flinched, too. Whatever she was hearing, it was getting louder.

"When she burned the tree house down, it was what we in psychiatry call a prenode, a quick surfacing of psychosis that often foreshadows the full-blown disease. It can happen in young women her age, and while it often passes quickly, when it comes back, it comes back with a vengeance." He nodded toward Sophie. "This one isn't going to pass without medical help."

"Fine, then we'll bring the hospital to her. You can come stay with us. I'll pay you double. Triple."

"Dianne—"

"You'd have your own living quarters, an entire wing of the house. Your only job would be Sophie."

"I can't do that. I want to do everything I can for her, but—" He thought of his own practice, just beginning. He thought of Dana and what she might need in terms of the future if she pulled through. He thought of his mother and what she might need. Suddenly, he felt a little ill himself, as if the corners of the ceiling that Sophie so feared were also closing in on him, and it must have shown on his face because Dianne dropped her head, resigned. "She needs around-the-clock medical care right now until she's able to come up from this, then she'll need careful management. This is a disease, Dianne. She's going to have to manage it for the rest of her life. And so will you."

Dianne laughed sadly, her mouth cut into a grimace.

"Careful management. Our family has always been good at that. It's what we do. Carry on as if nothing is ever wrong."

"That's not what I mean at all—"

"No hospitals. That's my right. I'm her legal guardian. I'm the final say. That's it. I'll care for her at home myself until this passes."

She was right. A child psychiatrist could only advise a path of treatment. He couldn't have anyone committed against the wishes of their legal guardians without tangible evidence of intent to harm. He didn't have that. And as much as he ground his teeth, he couldn't even hate Dianne for her decision. Gordon despised mental hospitals. Even the most luxurious of them treated the symptoms, not the cause. The more expensive the care, the more daintily they approached the root of the problem. Hospitals were businesses first and foremost.

But Dianne still didn't get that what Sophie had wasn't going to "pass." He didn't want her taking Sophie in her current state. He imagined she had looked very similar before she set fire to the tree house and before she disappeared last night—before Dana ended up on the grass, blood in her hair, her lips parted with eyes closed...

All Gordon could do was watch as Dianne gathered her daughter. Her touch was gentle but firm, and Sophie responded to it in her daze. He thought of Sophie and Dianne, alone in that massive house. He'd come to his senses about handing her over to the cops, only to watch his patient be carted off to a prison of another kind. Desperate, he took another tack.

"The police are already involved, Dianne. The explosion last night badly hurt an officer I care about. Her superior is directly involved, too. A man named Warren Duke."

Dianne paused. Gordon watched her carefully. She

brushed Sophie's damp hair from her forehead, trying to catch her daughter's rolling gaze with her own direct one. Gordon waited and listened, but Dianne was in no rush to explain herself.

Gordon chimed in again. "I've run across Duke in the past. He can be a... difficult man."

Dianne nodded but offered nothing more. Instead, she set her mouth in a prim line and helped Sophie to stand. When she looked at Gordon again, she was composed, as if she knew she had the upper hand.

"You care for my daughter. You want to see her well. I know it. So you'll have to work within the rules I've set. And you will. I know that too. That means no hospitals. No clinics. No outside opinions. Nothing without my say. I will call you when Sophie is well enough once more to continue her sessions."

Gordon moved aside as Dianne herded Sophie through the office and out the door, covering her with her own jacket to keep the soft but steady rain off her head until she disappeared once more into their waiting sedan.

After they left, Gordon poured himself a drink and sat on the floor with his back against the patient's couch. The clock ticked. The rain fell. Traffic hummed distantly. The day continued into night, and the full weight of what had occurred pressed upon him with slow, relentless pressure. His head felt heavy, but his eyes remained open. They followed along with the steps of his thoughts as he recounted each session he'd had with Sophie. He looked for missteps he might have made, missteps that had ended up with Dana in the hospital. He badly wanted someone to blame—might as well be himself.

But he couldn't see where he'd gone wrong. He'd done everything by the book. No psychiatrist he knew would have diagnosed schizophrenia right off the bat. Her symptoms were indicative of a psychotic break in some ways but atypical in others, especially Mo. Mo was in line with dissociative-identity disorder, which was very different from schizophrenia. Moreover, she wasn't responding to the benzos. The pills should have been enough to calm her by then.

He'd done the best he could with what he knew as he knew it, but he still felt that he hadn't acted quickly enough, that he *still* wasn't acting quickly enough to stave off the next disaster. Instead, he'd handed a very sick girl off to her mother, who sometimes seemed to value her family name more than her daughter. Gordon did believe that Dianne loved Sophie, in her own way—his own mother had strange ways of showing affection, too—but Dianne seemed willfully ignorant of her daughter's situation. She had managed to let the girl sneak out twice, and twice things had ended in flames—three times if you counted the tree out back.

Gordon picked up his phone and dialed Marty.

"You want me to bring her in?" he asked, first thing.

"No."

Marty was eating something—probably those damn almonds again—but he paused. "You're kidding me, right?"

"No. Something else is going on here. Sophie is too fragile. I can't risk being wrong."

"Then we figure out what else is going on while she sits in a holding cell, away from the matches. We hold kids all the time. You shoulda seen some of the goons I brought in from working the corners. It's no big deal."

Gordon could tell that Marty was still fired up. He knew Marty was the type of guy that went ice cold to deal with the moment and make a level decision, but he saved his anger for afterward. To keep himself going. To finish the job.

"She's not a drug dealer, Marty."

"She could have killed Dana," Marty said, popping each word.

"You think I don't know that?" Gordon asked, surprised to find himself yelling. "You think that wasn't on my mind the whole time she was here? But nothing about this case fits. When I was at her house, responding to the text, I saw Warren Duke there."

"Duke? You never told me that. Did he see you?"

"No. I don't think so. The explosion caught everyone's attention first."

Marty crunched another almond, slowly that time, as if in thought. "Warren Duke. What the hell?"

"I don't know. I'm not sure that Dianne knows, either. But she didn't seem worried when I told her he was involved. This goes beyond Sophie."

"So we just let her go about her merry way, then? Until she lights the whole frickin' town up?"

"No. I had to let her go with her mom, Dianne. And between you and me, I think Dianne's parental priorities are all out of whack. I see this quite a bit with parents in her tax bracket. Bottom line is I don't trust her to keep an eye on Sophie. The girl has slipped out three times now under Dianne's watch. I think we need to take over." He came to the decision as he spoke. He drained his scotch and found himself standing. Sleep would have to wait.

"Take over?" Marty asked.

"Yeah, we need to, ah..." Gordon searched for the right word, the cop word. "Case the joint."

Marty snorted.

"If we're right and she really is going to the school at

night, our best chance to catch her in the act is to nab her as she leaves home, right? Then I can walk her into round-the-clock care myself. With proof, what I say trumps Dianne. As a matter of fact, maybe you can arrest Dianne for criminal negligence while we're at it."

"Now we're talking," Marty said. "We use my car. I'll be over in twenty."

CHAPTER NINE

Gordon sat in silence with Marty, the two of them watching the house on Long Lane from the front seats of Marty's car. With the low rumble of the engine gone, the distance between the men seemed tangible. The name of that distance was *Dana*, but neither of them had addressed it yet.

Outside, the light was already starting to fail, and it seemed to lean heavily on everything it touched on its way out. The gold and red leaves hardly stirred on the trees. Those strewn upon the expansive grass lawns of the estates around them stuck there as if glued. Nobody walked the streets. No dogs barked. Gordon felt as if the entire neighborhood was standing in shock for the burned school five blocks down. He was reminded of the sleep laboratory at Johns Hopkins. The walls and ceilings of the control room there were covered in a strange, webbed material that caught and trapped all sound. He would have to take periodic breaks from the room when working because of how unsettling and heavy it felt.

"I meant to stop by Dana's place," Gordon said, clearing

his throat, speaking for the sake of breaking the silence. "Check on Chloe and Maria."

"I already did," Marty said, his hand hanging out the window, brushing the outside of his door. He didn't look at Gordon as he spoke. His eyes were focused intently on 8 Long Lane even as Gordon turned to look at him. "That a problem?" Marty asked. "I'm her partner. It's what partners do."

Gordon couldn't tell if he was trying to get a rise out of him or if he was just stating facts. Everything that came out of Marty's mouth sounded a bit like a challenge. Gordon wasn't one for confrontations. He preferred to nip things in the bud if they were awkward, to keep them from growing more so. So he said the first thing that came to his mind.

"It's a bit of a problem. Because I think you're in love with her."

Marty coughed. Gordon felt his face getting hot. The words had leapt from him before he could stop them. And more came behind.

"Chloe really likes you. I've seen it. At the promotion party, she practically jumped into your arms. And she hardly talks to me. Even though my job is talking to kids. Which tells me two things. One. Maybe I'm not as good at talking to kids as I think. And two, since I know Dana's a good person, odds are very high that Chloe is a good person, and if Chloe likes you, that means you are a good person. Kids can always tell. You're a good person, and you love my girlfriend, and you get to spend a lot of time with her. More than me. That doesn't bode well for me."

The silence that fell then was a palpable thing. Gordon cleared his throat to try to break it again, but it wouldn't be broken that time.

Whatever Marty had been expecting, it wasn't that. He creaked back in his seat. "Wow."

"Well, you asked me if I had a problem."

"Does all that"—Marty spun a finger near his temple —"go on in your head, like... all the time?"

"That's about a third of it, I'd say."

"Jesus."

"That's all you have to say?" Gordon asked. He gestured back and forth along the space between them. "Marty, we both are a big part of Dana's life. We've got to figure this out."

Marty's grip on the steering wheel tightened. He looked as though he was about to say something, but then he tensed suddenly and leaned forward, eyes intent.

"What is it?" Gordon asked.

Marty shoved a quieting hand in his face without looking and pointed down the curving lane. Gordon peered around his bulk, and there, at the very end, he saw a solitary figure in a plaid dress. The light from the street lamp above reflected dully off her long blond hair. Her arms were clutched around her chest, her back and head bowed, and she scanned the gutter as she walked, occasionally shaking her head.

Gordon muttered a soft curse.

"That's Sophie?" Marty asked.

"That's her."

"She looks awful," Marty said quietly.

"She feels awful."

They watched as Sophie sat down on the expansive front lawn of her neighbor's house, grabbed her bony knees, and started rocking. Gordon felt a physical pain in his chest at seeing her. As if his stomach was turning in slow knots. He wanted to run to her, console her, and give her a time and place and person she recognized in an attempt to ground her mind in the present. But if she was going to the school, on her way to burn again, they needed to know.

She was close enough that they should have been able to hear her if she'd been crying. Gordon listened intently until he realized she was being completely silent in her torment, as if she was trying to hide from the voices. From Mo.

"She doesn't look like she knows what planet she's on," Marty said. "Much less how to start a fire."

For five interminable minutes, they watched Sophie West spiral downward until she was practically flattened against the grass with the silent weight of her delusions. She never even made it past her neighbor's mailbox. Five minutes was all Gordon could take.

"This isn't helping anybody," he said, opening the door, ready to throw off Marty as best as he could if the big man protested.

Marty got out of the car after him, but to Gordon's surprise, he looked across the hood and waited. "She's in a nightmare right now. You just gonna stand there?"

Gordon tucked in his shirt and started walking. He felt beset on all sides by fears and insecurities—Dana and Marty, his mother and her cancer, his fledgling practice. In many ways, the cornerstones of his life were crumbling. But he could still help Sophie. This was what he did. This was his domain—maybe his last, but it was still his. With every step he took across the street, he stood a shade straighter. Marty seemed to understand as well. He followed several paces behind Gordon, giving him the lead.

Gordon took even and sure steps until he was able to sit down in front of Sophie on the grass. He did this without speaking, and he kept a relaxed and receptive look on his face, as if nothing was remotely odd about the two of them sitting on a freshly cut lawn in the chill of an October night.

Sophie looked at him in stride. She didn't jump or shy away, but she didn't recognize him either. Gordon knew that by then, Sophie most likely had built him into her delusions in some way. Whether they were in the patient's chair or on the front lawn hardly mattered to her.

"Hi, Sophie," he said.

"You're here to kill me."

"No, Sophie. I'm here to help you, like the other times."

"Then I'm here to kill you," she said, nodding slowly to herself.

Gordon fought against a shiver. "Nobody is killing anyone, Sophie," he said calmly. He purposely repeated her name again and again, to remind her of who she was.

Sophie shook her head pityingly. "If I don't, everyone dies worse. In pain forever. All the way down the line. Burning now saves them later. Except..."

Gordon waited, but Sophie seemed to have lost her thought. "Except what, Sophie?"

"Except that I can't do it. I can't save you." She sobbed quietly, rocking again.

"That's okay. I don't need to be sav—"

"But Mo does what I can't," she whispered, staring at him with cold, wide eyes that froze the words in his mouth. "Mo can save you. Mo can clean you."

Gordon saw his opportunity. "Does Mo want to talk to me right now?"

Sophie looked around rapidly. She checked the shadows carefully and listened to the sky. "Later," she whispered. "He'll come for you later."

Gordon nodded, but he was troubled. Her symptoms had danced around one another like waves in a stormy bay, but they were violently colliding, and Gordon couldn't parse one from the other. All was one wave.

Sophie was shivering. The wind picked up and kicked tiny locust leaves in a swirl around her. They caught in her hair and rattled down the concrete like scattered toothpicks.

"Let's go home, Sophie," Gordon said.

Sophie nodded, but she stayed in a ball until Gordon gently led her to stand, with a sure grip on her elbow. Protocol had gone out the window some time before.

Marty followed at a distance while Gordon took Sophie up the winding flagstone front path of 8 Long Lane. He found the door open and didn't bother knocking.

"Dianne," he called from the foyer, working with effort to keep his voice steady and even. "It's me, Gordon Pope." *Again.*

Silence.

"I found Sophie. She's right here. She's okay." He turned to Sophie and found her already staring at him, not in alarm, but with intensity. "You're okay," he repeated to her.

The house was as silent as when he'd first visited. All he heard was the ticking of an enormous grandfather clock he couldn't see and the soft whistle of his lungs pulling air as he tried to keep calm.

"Sophie, is your mom here?"

She still stared at him like an infant, offering little. He felt she was hardly daring to breathe, as if any movement might betray her location to Mo and the voices she thought were chasing her.

He turned around and found Marty watching him carefully as well, from just outside the door, with an intensity of a different sort.

"I'm gonna find Dianne," Gordon said.

"Open door's an open door," Marty said quietly. "And I've had about enough of this shit. But let's make it quick." He moved around Gordon with an eye to the hallways on the ground floor and the kitchen beyond.

Gordon led Sophie to the stairs. She needed a safe space, a place she'd already cleaned and ordered—her bedroom—and he guessed that was somewhere upstairs. She moved in quick, birdlike jerks, and a subtle whine gathered at the base of her throat. He picked up the pace but stopped at the bottom step. Hand-drawn pictures were strewn about the stairway from top to bottom, perhaps twenty of them, some flat, others crumpled, some at odd angles against the banister. One hanging precariously from the carpeted runner three steps above fluttered down to the ground at Gordon's feet as if disturbed by a ghost's passing. A quick glance showed the same table-on-fire pencil drawing as the one Dianne had given him.

"Did you do this, Sophie?" Gordon asked, picking up the nearest drawing.

She didn't seem to see any of them or much of anything in front of her. She was muttering to herself in sibilants, soft hissing sounds that reminded Gordon of hidden pockets of air escaping burning logs. Marty came back in from the kitchen and found Gordon's eyes. The big man shook his head. Nobody was on the first floor. So up they went.

Gordon picked up the pictures at each step, gripping them in a tattered portfolio with his free hand. He could hear Marty following several steps behind, his heavy work boots pressing the carpeted runner as he walked.

"Dianne!" Gordon called again, as loudly as he dared with Sophie on his arm.

He listened, and then he thought he heard something. Steps. Small steps, pattering in a quick run and then stopping. So fast he almost couldn't be sure what he'd heard. He turned around and found Marty listening with his head cocked. He'd heard something too.

"Dianne, it's Gordon, I've brought Sophie. I'm here with a... a friend." Gordon stepped faster, reached the landing between floors and then turned toward the second floor. At the top was a bedroom with double doors wide open. As Gordon crested the stairs, he saw quick flashes of light coming from a television there, staccato bursts that lit the darkened room like a strobe, and in the glimpses he was given, he saw a lump of bunched blankets, and from the lump a hand draped, fingertips trailing nearly to the ground.

"Dianne?"

No movement. Gordon stepped quickly to the doors and paused. Dianne West was sprawled out on an enormous bed, the covers bunched oddly around her body and head. For a horrible span of seconds, Gordon thought she was dead, but then she unleashed an enormous snore that made him jump, almost yanking Sophie back. Even Marty flinched, waiting back at the stairs.

"Dianne, get up," Gordon said.

He slowly let go of Sophie, and once he was convinced she could stand on her own, he shook Dianne gently at the shoulders. She breathed heavily but wouldn't wake up. At the nightstand to her side was a fifth of vodka, three quarters empty, and a bottle of prescription pills. Sophie's prescription pills, the benzos. Gordon picked up the pill bottle, and its white cap fell right off. He feared the worst, that Dianne was in the process of trying to kill herself as they stood there, but the bottle was nearly full. Perhaps two or three pills were gone at most.

His initial relief was replaced quickly by a hardening anger. Dianne had never given Sophie her anxiety medication to begin with. She was stealing it herself, popping one or two at night with four or five shots of vodka as a sleepytime cocktail. No wonder Sophie got the run of the neighborhood. Dianne was maybe a hundred pounds soaking wet. A stampeding elephant wouldn't wake her at that point.

"In what world can I not have kids but you can," he muttered. He turned back to Marty. "She's been self-medicating. With Sophie's prescription."

Marty nodded, but he seemed distracted. He had one ear down the hallway. "You heard those footsteps, right?" he asked, his tone low, as if speaking to himself. "Somebody else might be here."

"There's nobody else here, Marty. This place is an enormous tomb. It could have been anything that we heard—a floorboard, the furnace, the pipes. But if I don't get Sophie to a safe place soon, the damage could take years to mend."

Sophie's fluttering heartbeat was visible through the pale white skin at her temple. She looked at him with pleading eyes. "You must be quiet," she whispered. "You must be quiet. Everyone be quiet. Everyone be quiet. They'll hear you. They'll hear you."

Repetition. Delusions. Not long now. Gordon rolled a pill into his palm and walked over to Dianne's work desk in the corner, where her computer idled. There, an empty glass stood next to a full pitcher of water. He smelled it to make sure then poured Sophie a glass and brought it to her. He was expecting her to fight it—no telling what she was seeing then or what she thought the water might be—but she took the pill down and the entire glass of water in a series of long gulps.

She gasped for breath at the end. "Will they go away now? Will they go away now?" Her voice wheezed.

"They'll go away soon."

The jostling of the desk snapped Dianne's computer awake, and it flicked on with a brightness that made Gordon squint. A wall of unbroken text appeared on the screen. Dianne's precious memoirs. He turned back toward her, motionless and snoring loudly through everything. He shook his head in disgust. *How can she possibly have so much to say?*

"C'mon Sophie," Gordon said, "let's get you to bed."

But Sophie had already settled into bed, on the opposite side of Dianne, curled up in a ball, staring at her mother across a space big enough to fit another two Sophies. Her muttering stopped. She seemed catatonic, but at least her breathing was calming—slow, exhausted gulps instead of panicked rabbit breaths.

"I want to take a quick look at the rest of this landing," Marty said slowly. "I swear I heard something—"

A sound came from downstairs, a slow, soft *whoosh* of air accompanied by the sure turning of oiled hinges. The front door was being opened again. Both men froze, staring at each other, then moved quickly and quietly to the banister over the landing.

Warren Duke took two sharp steps into the foyer. The clean clicking sound his gleaming oxford shoes made on the wood seemed to echo around the entire house. Gordon stared like a cow over the railing until Marty whipped him back out of view.

"Dianne," Duke said, his voice clear and commanding. "Sophie, get down here."

Gordon turned to Marty dumbly, mouth working in silence, until the big man's crushing grip on both shoulders steadied him.

Marty leaned in close and whispered, "We have to find another way out."

Gordon looked to his left and right. He looked up, to the darkened third floor. He looked behind him, to the room where Dianne still snored and the manic light of the television played off Sophie's unblinking eyes as she stared at her mother. Nothing looked like an exit.

"Dianne, if I have to come up there, it's not going to go well for you or Sophie," Duke said.

Gordon heard two more sharp steps toward the base of the stairs. He looked at Marty and shook his head, helpless. His bowels felt loose and roiling. He was sure Duke could hear his stomach, even over Dianne's snoring.

"Goddammit, Dianne!" Duke said. "Do you want the police to take Sophie?" Another sharp step, then a soft step. The first stair. Another. Faster. He was coming up two at a time.

Gordon pulled Marty in that time. "Hide," he whispered. He pushed Marty away from him, down the hall, then turned and stepped as carefully and quickly as he could the other direction. Gordon crept until he found the library, darkened. It smelled oddly of campfire—or perhaps he just had fire on the brain. He contemplated closing the door but knew he had no time to hide the click of the lock. Across the hall, Marty stepped into what looked like a linen closet, large enough to be a bathroom. Marty swung the door closed behind him, stopping at the latch, just as Warren Duke stepped onto the second-floor landing.

Gordon had a bull's-eye view of the man from where he stood in the darkness. He was dressed in gray slacks and a navy sport coat with golden buttons that gleamed even in the low light. He was tanned to perfection, his salt-and-pepper hair cut short, just a shade longer than a military buzz. His jacket was trim and fitted, save for a slight bump under the right armpit, a gun.

As soon as Duke had walked through the front door, Gordon's mind fled down the path of every worst-case scenario he could think of, from getting thrown out to getting in a fistfight with the major, even getting arrested. Seeing the gun reminded him that things could always be worse. If things went really south that night, he could end up dead. His stomach squeaked again. Duke didn't notice. He was looking into the open bedroom, and his eyes were angry slits. By then, he'd seen the bed, but if he felt shock or dismay, he didn't show it—only sneering disgust.

"Sophie," he said. Another command. He put his hands on his hips, as though he was scolding an unruly dog. He took a step toward the bed, almost out of Gordon's line of sight, when the closet Marty hid within suddenly clicked. Nothing remarkable. Not an opening. Not a closing. Just a latching, as if the tongue of the handle had finally decided to shoot into the lock.

But Warren Duke heard it.

Duke rocked backward on his heel, looking down the hallway toward Marty.

"Who's there?" he said, low, growling. His eyes fell on the closed closet. He turned toward it and slid his handgun from its shoulder holster with the sound of metal on leather.

Without knowing quite why, without any real reason, other than the knowledge that things would go much worse for Marty, in the long run, than they would for him if one of the two of them were caught, Gordon stepped forward from the library into the light.

"It's me, Duke. It's Gordon Pope."

Duke spun around in an instant, and Gordon grimaced, waiting for the roar of the gun and the ripping of bullets.

Two of them. Maybe three, tearing his stomach to pieces—at least it would shut the growling up. But no shots came.

When Gordon opened his eyes again, he saw a strange thing. He saw a hint of fear in Warren Duke's face, but the gun never wavered. And Gordon knew that the only thing more dangerous than a furious man was a frightened furious man.

"I've been treating Sophie," Gordon said slowly, his hands out and up at shoulder height. "I found her outside, wandering alone. She's having an attack. I believe that she's schizophrenic and that there's a good chance she's been setting fires, listening to the voices in her head. I just wanted to make sure she was safe in here and not... out there."

Warren stared at Gordon the entire time he spoke. The vein at his right temple pulsed. When Gordon finished, Duke stayed still. Only a brief twitch of his right eye betrayed that he'd processed Gordon's words at all.

"Are you alone?" Duke asked, his voice a low growl.

"Yes," Gordon said, making a huge effort not to glance behind Duke at the closet. "And now that you're here and you can take things over, I'll leave. Like I said, I just wanted to make sure she wasn't..."

"Lighting fires," Duke said evenly. "Like the one that nearly killed Detective Frisco." His face was hard and his eyes flinty, showing no remorse—certainly not for Dana personally, but also not even for a fallen fellow officer. Not for anything.

"You can put the gun down, Duke. I'm not gonna hurt anybody."

Far from putting the gun down, Duke walked toward Gordon slowly. "I can't be sure of that," he said. "I get a message about a little girl wandering the neighborhood, and

I find you hiding here with her. I don't know what your intentions are."

He stopped with the gun inches from Gordon's forehead. It seemed to suck in the weak light from the hallway, its dull black gleam fading into the darkness around them. Gordon could smell Duke's cologne and hear his even breathing.

"You can ask Dianne—"

"Don't talk about Dianne!" Duke snapped, stunning Gordon into silence. "Why is it that every time there is an issue in my district that requires my attention, I find you feeding in the mud at the bottom of it?"

"I don't know," Gordon said honestly. He was wondering that himself. He'd been thrown into a cage with Duke twice now in a span of as many months. That didn't seem fair to either of them.

"Do you think I need help doing my job, Pope?"

Sometimes. But he bit off the reply and shook his head vigorously. "Nope. You do your job, and I do mine."

"What was *your* job—Sophie and her episodes—is now *my* job. Mine alone. Do you understand me?"

Gordon backed up a step, eyeing Duke sidelong. "Are you telling me not to treat my patient?"

"This is police business now. You can either turn it over to me, or I can make you turn it over to me. Are we clear?"

"Not really. I'm treating Sophie at Dianne's request, not yours—"

Duke stepped in to Gordon, closing the space between them quickly. He wrapped Gordon in a bear hug with his free arm and shoved the barrel of his gun up and under Gordon's chin, digging into the soft skin there until he almost choked. Gordon saw a flutter of movement from the closet beyond and shook his head quickly. The door paused.

"I understand now," Gordon said, his voice thin and strained, his Adam's apple bouncing off the cold steel of the barrel. "I understand," he croaked again.

Duke stepped off, holstered his gun in one deft movement, then picked at the cuffs of his light-pink oxford until satisfied with how far they protruded from his jacket sleeves. He smiled wanly, as if he'd never attacked Gordon at all.

"I'm going to escort you out of this house now, Pope, and if I ever see you near Sophie again, I'm opening a sex-offender investigation. It will follow you around your entire life and destroy what little practice you have. Not many people want to trust their children with a sex-offender psychiatrist."

"I'm not a sex offender, Duke," Gordon said, surprised at the growl in his voice.

"Oh, I know that. You're a third wheel, a thorn in my side. You take real police off of real work, and you insert yourself where you're not wanted. Constantly. But I'm fairly sure you're not a sex offender. That hardly matters, though, does it? Once the claim is made, the taint is on you regardless."

Gordon swallowed hard. He knew Duke was right.

"I see you do understand. Now, then. You first."

Duke walked behind Gordon as they descended the stairs. Gordon took his time crossing the great room, hoping that Marty would find that back exit they'd been looking for before Duke came back up.

Duke shoved him in the back. "Move it."

After another shove, Gordon was out of the house. The big door swung shut behind him and locked. Gordon shivered, his sweat-soaked collar and brow chilled in the cold night air. He walked down the winding path and across the street before he turned to see the house again. The center-front window on the second floor was for the master bedroom. He watched the distant flicker of the television as he tried to piece together what had just happened. Duke had come on strong—so strong he'd nearly shot him, which was very unlike Warren Duke. That would've created far too messy a cleanup, even for a major. The slow ruination of Gordon's life with a false sex-offender accusation was more Duke's speed, maybe with a pistol whip thrown in there for good measure. Either way, one thing was for sure: something about this case meant an awful lot to Warren Duke. Gordon recalled the flash of fear in his eyes. *What about Sophie could possibly scare a man like Warren Duke?*

After a few minutes, the light in the master bedroom went on, and Gordon saw Duke from the waist up. He moved over to the bed and shook someone, hopefully Dianne. He was not gentle.

"You weren't kidding," Marty whispered from nearby. He was walking down the sidewalk toward him, breathing heavily and edging toward the lawn.

If Gordon had had any adrenaline left, he might have yelped and brought Duke to the window. He'd given Marty little to no hope of escape, fully expecting to see the major screaming at the detective through the window next.

"Duke is elbow deep in all this," Marty said.

"Jesus, Marty. After all that, you think it's a good idea to sneak up on a guy?"

"You'll live."

"How'd you get out?"

"Through the bedroom. It's a huge his-and-hers deal. At the back, there's a door to that porch and a fire escape on the far side." Marty pointed to the right of the second story, where a whitewashed porch wrapped around the far edge.

"Good thing."

"Yeah. Good thing. Listen, I, uh…" He struggled with his words and cleared his throat softly. "Thanks for saving my ass in there. You didn't have to do that. Not after all I said about you."

"What did you say about me?" Gordon asked.

"You know, in the car. And… other stuff. I'm just sayin' you didn't have to." His voice was soft. Marty had spoken quietly before, but never softly.

"Yeah, well. Duke actually has to go a step out of his way to ruin my life. He can ruin yours in his sleep."

Both men watched as Duke helped Sophie to sitting. They could just barely see the top of her head as he sat next to her. She was bobbing, looking toward the ceiling, and he turned her face back to his again and again as he spoke intently. Gordon took some small comfort in the fact that at least she seemed remarkably unperturbed at seeing Duke.

"He's kind of a piece of shit, isn't he?" Marty said softly. "The major."

"Yes, he is, Marty. Yes, he is." *And I wish I knew why.*

Back in the library, Gordon had had his stomach in his shoes and his hands in the air with Duke's gun in his face, yet he still couldn't quite believe he was seeing the man. Duke was right: they kept running into each other. And each time, Duke seemed more disposed to hate him. He'd claimed Gordon was meddlesome, but nobody holds a meddlesome man at gunpoint. Duke was another puzzle piece. Part of the greater picture. Gordon was determined to figure where he fit.

In the quiet silence, as both men watched Duke try and fail to put Sophie straight, Gordon thought for the first time that while he and Marty would never be friends, maybe they could help each other figure out the common thread.

Marty turned his head a tick to the right. His eyes were intent again, like an elk catching a sound.

Gordon followed his gaze to the second level, just outside the master bedroom, where the porch wrapped around the second deck. "What is it?" he asked.

"I thought I saw something," Marty said, all softness gone, his voice slate again.

"Where, on the porch?"

"Shut up."

They watched for another half minute. Nothing.

"I don't see anything, Marty." But as he spoke, his words died in the air.

A small figure in a white T-shirt and a black hat appeared on the deck with exaggerated, prancing steps, and as he did, Gordon was struck by how wrong he had been about everything he'd assumed. Flat wrong. As wrong as he could be.

Gordon drew a singular line of sight from where Warren Duke was still speaking to Sophie on the bed where Dianne snored, to the outside of the window, across the second story, to where Mo stood with his hands on his hips, grinning hugely in the moonlight. He saw them looking. He looked right back and put one finger to his lips.

Everything went out of the window. In more ways than one.

"Son of a bitch," Marty said, bewildered.

If Gordon could speak, he would have agreed.

CHAPTER TEN

Dana hovered in a world in between. She felt as if she were in several places at once—some small part of her knew she was in a hospital bed, attached at the arms and hands and mouth to tubes and machines, but she was not there on the inside. She had no sense of time. She felt no pain. In the place her mind inhabited, the touch of the thin hospital sheets lay upon her with as much presence as shadows. The rhythmic hiss and beep of the machines were like white noise. She was in a hospital bed, but she was not *mostly* in a hospital bed.

Dana was *mostly* walking back and forth over a well-worn path in her brain: the minutes leading up to the explosion that had burrowed a piece of gas-soaked metal into her brain just above the temple. At first, she was running up and down that path, and she was helpless to stop herself. She relived the explosion again and again, each time recognizing her fate too late, seeing that the trail of flame she followed led to a pile of stinking gas canisters, which exploded again and again and again in a flash of white heat that obliterated her and put her back at the beginning again, on the lawn outside the lab, in the dead of night, tracing a snaking trail of fire.

She felt no pain when she was obliterated, only panic. The experience repeated itself faster than she could sort it out properly in the compartments of her brain. She felt like a woman picking a single apple from a tree, only to find another behind it, then ten, then a hundred more falling around her.

For all Dana knew, she relived the explosion for years. Or perhaps just for moments. Time had lost all effect upon her. She lived in a vacuum of personal tragedy until one time, when she was deposited at the start again, instead of running after the flame as she had forever, she walked.

The snake of flame didn't run away from her. It kept pace just ahead. She couldn't stamp it out, nor could she dash to catch it, but she found she was able to conduct it, rewinding and playing and fast-forwarding, as if she was at the controls.

Dana no longer felt panic once she was at the controls, but she did get angry. The damn fuse was always out of her reach, like a carrot in front of a donkey. She swiped, spat, and screamed at it. Nothing worked. Sometimes, she became so infuriated at her impotence that she sped everything up again and took off running as she had in the beginning, just so she could explode along with her frustration.

She always ended up at the beginning. On the lawn, in the moonlight, the fuse just out of reach.

Other times, Dana sat on the grass of the darkened schoolyard right at the beginning and did nothing but watch the flame. When she stood still and it stood still, the fuse looked less like the instrument of her demise and more like a candle in a dark window.

She might have sat for moments. Or for years. Or forever.

Only one other person joined her on that well-worn path of her brain: the fire starter. The one who lit the fuse. And whoever he was, he inhabited the farthest edge of what had become her world. Just close enough to exist. Mere steps from falling off the map.

Dana spent swaths of what passed for time in that place watching the fire starter. He moved just like the fire, locked on a predestined path, in perfect timing with everything else. At first, she thought he'd never be more than a mirage in the distance, but after a time,

Dana found a single frozen moment along the inevitable path to her explosion where she could see his eyes. That frozen heartbeat was very near the end, very close to the obliterating whiteness. She was fully inside the darkened, hollowed science lab, but the fuse hadn't yet reached the canisters. In that frozen moment, inches from oblivion, the boy stood nearly visible. The brim of his hat still obscured the top of his head, and the shadows obscured the bottom half, but his eyes were visible in a single stripe of light from the fuse, like a superhero's mask. That was when he'd looked back at Dana. That was when their eyes met, just before the explosion.

The fire starter was frozen, crouched to run, shoulders thrust forward. He looked eager to go but torn on which way to run. Half of him was set to flee the blast, but the other half looked as though it wanted to run toward it, as if he wanted the oblivion too.

In the fey light of the fuse, Dana couldn't tell the color of his eyes, but it was obvious that they were in pain. Floating as they were, between two strips of shadow on his face, Dana was able to take them out of that well-worn path entirely—away from the fire and the white that followed—and when she did, when she focused only on them, she thought they looked more afraid than triumphant, more tormented than pleased.

Dana wanted desperately to know more. She felt very close to understanding the child, very close to knowing who he was, but her brain had offered all it could in terms of the past. Already, it was growing restless with itself, changing things Dana knew for fact with machinations of its own. Toying with her. The fire starter's face became Chloe's. Then her mom's face. Gordon's. Her own. Each more silent and staring than the last, until she couldn't take it anymore and ran into the blinding white explosion again

The loop was enough to make anyone crazy. She felt herself spiraling slowly downward into a place of no return. She knew of a way to make the white at the end last longer. To jump the well-worn path altogether. It involved giving up, no longer caring what was beyond where she was trapped. Easy enough to do. She supposed, although she dared not dwell on it, that she could fall *completely* into the white—leave the loop, and everything else, forever. She admitted to herself that the notion held appeal. Like when she caught herself falling a touch too far into a daydream. It would be so easy, like falling backward. All she had to do was decide to do it. And since in that place, dwelling upon the white was the same as inviting it in, she suddenly found herself walking to the explosion. Pausing right before. Turning around, closing her eyes. She held her arms out, ready to fall into the whiteness forever...

Then she heard Gordon's voice.

"We're on the same case again," he said. *"You and I. I thought you might want to know that. Your fire starter is my patient's imaginary friend. Maybe if I told you at dinner.*

Talked more. Was present more. Maybe we could have figured out that we're on the same road and could've tackled this together. Maybe then I wouldn't have been so sloppy."

Dana dropped her arms to her side and retreated from the explosion. The flame backtracked with her. "We still can, Gordon. I'm here. I'm right here."

"I owe it to Sophie to figure this out. And I owe it to you, too."

"You don't owe me anything, Gordon," she said, speaking to the black sky within her mind. "You've already given enough. Maybe too much."

"So how about this? How about if I don't give up, you don't give up. Deal?"

"Deal."

Gordon sighed, and it sounded like the wind whispering through the giant tree under which Dana found herself sitting once more.

"Now I just gotta find an imaginary friend that starts fires," she heard Gordon say. He sounded heartbroken. He sounded the way the fire starter's eyes looked, which was how she came to understand.

"Look for loss, Gordon. Look for loss and for pain, and you'll find your imaginary friend. You'll find your fire starter," she said, but her words were carried away into the blackness above.

"Remember our deal, now. Okay? Please?"

"I'll remember."

GORDON WATCHED Dana carefully in the silence, not expecting any answer, of course, but willing to at least give her a chance.

Nothing.

Nothing but the slow hiss of the ventilator and the continuous beeping of her vitals. Gordon had been by Dana's side for only ten minutes, and the sounds were already driving him crazy. *If anything gets through to her, it's gonna be that damn beeping, not me.*

He sat back on the couch, rested his head on top of its back, and stared at the mauve ceiling. Mauve walls. Mauve floors. Even the couch he sat on, the kind that was halfway between couch and awkward single-sleeper bed, seemed different shades of mauve. Gordon started to drift in a sea of mauve. He'd been awake for almost two days straight. He felt the autumn sun drifting through the window and draping across his face like warm lace. He didn't want to look at it. Another morning had come, and he was no closer to figuring out how to help the people he was supposed to help—farther, in fact. Dana might just sleep forever. And if she did, he was resolved to sleep forever too. Maybe they'd run into each other somewhere out there, forever sleeping.

GORDON AWOKE TO A TAPPING, light but insistent, on his knee. Pain shot through his neck, and his mouth felt gritty, his tongue foreign. He rolled it around his closed mouth to no avail as he righted his eyeglasses and realized with a sinking feeling that he was still in the hospital. Dana was still motionless in the bed in front of him. Everything was the same except that Chloe was at his side, tapping his knee.

Gordon coughed to clear his throat and scooted quickly to make way for the girl. He checked his watch—just past eight in the morning. He'd conked out for almost two hours, just long enough to feel terrible when awoken.

"Hi, Chloe," he said hoarsely.

Maria stood at the foot of Dana's bed. She glanced at

him but didn't seem to see him. She was completely absorbed by her silent and still daughter, as if she was seconds from collapsing onto Dana's bed herself. She had the heartbreaking look of the elderly in grief, as if all of the strength she had stored up to face her own end had to be used prematurely to face another untimely end. She was pallid and gray, years older than she had been two days before.

Chloe was different. Gordon was all too familiar with the unique ways children dealt with grief. Kids played the hands they were dealt. They knew no better. Adults complained about the hand while kids figured out how best to play.

"Did you sleep here all night?" Chloe asked. Her face was streaked with tears, but they were old tears, and they clashed oddly with her bright eyes and casual tone. She made no move to sit next to him.

"Not all night. Just for a bit," Gordon said.

Chloe nodded understandingly. "I try to sleep here, but Gigi says it's not good for me." She looked conspiratorially at Maria, who had moved over to Dana's other side and was gently massaging her right hand.

"Do you talk to Mom?" Chloe asked.

"Yeah."

"Me too. Did she answer?"

"No."

"Me neither."

Chloe held her favorite book at her side, the one Dana read to her nightly. *Just in case,* Gordon thought. Chloe stood in stark contrast to everything in that room. Optimistic. Inquisitive. Awake. Even her bright-pink tracksuit seemed to push back against the mauve and fight against Dana's coma in some subconscious way. She watched her mom carefully, and those bright eyes turned brighter again with unshed tears, but Chloe didn't fight them or wallow in them. Perhaps she had, at first, but since then had learned that tears had no better chance of waking her mother than dry eyes.

Maria busied herself tidying a room that didn't need tidying, plucking a few dead stems from the single vase of flowers at the sink, which looked hospital standard. No other cards sat nearby. No other flowers. No teddy bears holding little hearts that said Get Well Soon! Cops nearly killed in the line of duty got national news, an outpouring from the department and community, but all that was missing, and although Gordon didn't know *how*, he was confident the strange hush surrounding Dana was due to Warren Duke. He could almost smell the man's cologne underneath it all.

"That tube is helping her breathe," Chloe said knowingly. She took a few deep breaths, as if to prove to herself that she still didn't need one of her own.

"I'm sorry, Chloe," Gordon said suddenly. His role in all of this, in Dana ending up there, hung on him like the invisible film of a bad hangover. Maria stopped her plucking, and by the slight turn in her head, Gordon knew she was looking for someone to blame, too... and finding him. Gordon understood. In the few months he'd been dating her daughter, she and Dana had gone from the frying pan to the fire. He felt as though he were sinking down in the couch with the weight of her eyes.

Chloe tapped him on the knee again, concerned, not for Dana but for him.

"It's okay. You didn't hurt Mom," she said simply—a mantra, perhaps one Maria taught her as she was trying to explain tragedy to the little girl, and she had given it to Gordon.

Gordon found it incredible that Chloe would even acknowledge him when her mother was on ventilation three feet away, much less try to cheer him up. He smiled, and a bit of the weight that had settled on him shifted off, dropping to the floor.

"Do you know who did hurt her?" Chloe asked, and the evenness in her voice, the sudden and slight distance, hammered home to Gordon that the young girl really was her mother's daughter. She wanted justice.

"Sort of," Gordon said. That was all he could think to truthfully say.

Chloe nodded again, as though the two of them were on the case. Just talking to the girl made Gordon feel better by the minute.

"Are you gonna get them?" Chloe asked quietly. "You and Mister M?"

Mister M was Chloe's name for Marty. She thought he and Marty were a pair, which made Gordon smile and made him miss Dana all the more acutely, like a stitch in his side. Dana was trying her best to bring Gordon to Marty's level in her daughter's eyes, and it seemed to be working.

"I'm gonna try," Gordon said. He didn't know how and wasn't even confident he could get himself through the morning, but he would try.

Gordon stood and picked up his briefcase. He stretched his neck again and walked on pins and needles to the door. He paused by Maria, and she nodded farewell, eyes downcast. She closed the door softly behind him, and he was left in the hushed hallway. He walked without direction down the halls, around corners, through heavy double doors—

walking just to walk, walking to wake his brain. Soon enough, his mind fell back to the facts, the puzzle pieces.

Sophie was not Mo. Mo was not Sophie. That meant Gordon had to figure out who Mo was. Obviously, he was someone with ties to Sophie. Someone that knew the house on Long Lane or had access to it. Someone who had known Sophie for a long time. Mo had been a fixture of Sophie's life since she was a little girl. Gordon wondered if he'd always been real. If he had, more questions presented themselves—like how he could remain a boy for over a decade. And how the rest of the family could have missed him for all those years.

Gordon checked his watch. Time to make a family visit of his own.

When he walked into his mother's room, she was already awake. Her gauntness pained him. She looked off-color as well, and he could tell by the slight pinch to her mouth that the radiation therapy of the day before was making her ill, but she still smiled at him. "It's my son!" she said, as if he'd flown in from out of town.

The *Sun* was already read, set on the chair, and she was halfway through the *Wall Street Journal*. She turned down her page and set the paper to one side, looking at him squarely.

"How are you, Gordon?"

"Not good. But you're worse, and I feel like an ass talking about me."

"Oh, nonsense," she said, waving his comment away. "Aside from the cancer, I'm just fine."

He was acutely aware of a lack of soft chiming to her movement. Her usual jewelry was off and away. She had a plastic ID bracelet instead, flush to her wrist and comically small. He badly missed her chimes.

Gordon dropped his briefcase to the floor and sat on the couch opposite his mother's bed. He felt he was living out of a briefcase those days, from couch to couch. He couldn't help noticing the couch in his mother's room was a lot plusher and a lot less plastic than the one in Dana's. And more brightly colored. Mauve had no place in the out-of-pocket suites. The beeps and hisses of the machines were hushed there as well, hidden behind walls and curtains, away from view.

"Can we get Dana up here?" Gordon asked.

"Would it matter to her?" his mother asked.

Gordon scratched at the four-day-old growth of beard beginning to itch his neck. "No," he said, "I suppose not. She'd say she was just fine with the rest of the world downstairs. If she could."

His mother folded her hands in her lap and waited for Gordon to speak. The bed was folded tightly around her, but the only evidence of her bottom half were the two small points of her knees. She seemed to be shrinking by the hour, which wasn't good, going into a major surgery. Ideally, she would be hale and hearty. Ideally, the surgical team should be worried about giving her enough anesthesia to knock her out. Instead, Gordon was sure they feared the opposite: that they would give her too much and she might not awaken.

"What happened?" she asked after half a minute, during which Gordon didn't take the bait. "You only stare at the ceiling like that when you're feeling more forlorn than usual."

"You know Sophie's imaginary friend? The voice in her telling her to start fires?"

"Yes," Deborah replied, playing along.

"Turns out he's not imaginary after all."

He waited for the gasp, the theatrics. Instead, his mother laughed delicately.

"So you were right, after all," she said.

"What? No, Mother. I was about as wrong as you could be. Mo isn't Sophie's psychotic delusion. Nor is he some personality of hers. He's as real as you and me."

"Forgive me. I thought you were trying to diagnose your patient. You know: do your job, not figure out who this Mo is."

Gordon didn't follow. "The two go hand in hand."

"Oh, so I suppose that now you know this Mo is a real person, everything is fine with your patient, then. She's back in school, is she?"

Gordon thought of Sophie checking the ceilings. Babbling. Washing. Her near catatonic state on the bed.

"No. She's very sick. And now that I think we can safely rule out dissociative identity disorder..."

"Your initial case for schizophrenia is that much stronger. Congratulations. Looks like you were correct. You have a full-blown schizophrenic patient with an impish firebug of a friend."

His mother was right. Sophie's symptoms exhibited themselves despite Mo, not because of him. He'd been so focused on catching Mo for Dana, and for himself, that he'd lost focus on helping Sophie. Mo wasn't his patient. Sophie was.

"So I was right about the schizophrenia. I left her worse off than when I started treating her. Forgive me if I don't break out the champagne on a correct diagnosis."

"You should break out the champagne anytime you have champagne, Gordon, but that's beside the point. The point is you're still thinking of this Mo person as part of Sophie's diagnosis. He's not."

Gordon opened up his battered leather satchel and took out the collection of drawings he'd found scattered along the stairs of the house on Long Lane. He eyed the topmost, taking in the table and the manic grin of Mo standing high atop the family.

"What is he, then?"

"Part of the treatment. Of course."

His mother's words seemed to cause a subtle shift in the ground under Gordon, as if by turning the puzzle upside-down, he might better find a place for the errant pieces he still held.

"She'll never have a cure. Schizophrenia carries with it a lifetime of symptom management," Deborah said. "She'll always be striving for balance and understanding of what triggers her breaks, what brings on episodes, what causes her anxiety. You said yourself Sophie and Mo are connected somehow, and as long as Mo is still out raising hell, she'll never be able to manage her condition. But if you straighten out Mo, it will go a long way to straightening out Sophie."

The shift grew more pronounced. His mother's words rang true. They also ran right up against Warren Duke's threats.

"Warren Duke wants me off this case. He threatened me with a phony sexual-assault inquiry."

"That man again?"

"Said he'd shut down my practice. He *really* doesn't want me to dig any deeper in this."

"I see." Deborah seemed to weigh sides in her mind, tilting her head this way and that. "And how does that make you feel?"

"Like I must be getting close to figuring out the whole picture," Gordon said, grinning.

"So you'll keep walking, then?"

"I'd never forgive myself if I stopped."

"Wonderful! You've moved past diagnosis and are now in treatment," she proclaimed, adding a little clap at the end.

Gordon flipped through the collected drawings, his mother's words still reverberating in his head. He felt lighter, so he stood. He took the drawings over to a two-seat table near the bay window and laid them out, end to end, as he might a CT scan of a brain, which in many ways, they were.

All day, he'd been looking for similarities between the pictures, but he decided to turn the puzzle upside-down. Now he noticed differences. Consistent differences.

Always Mo, standing above the table—always Sophie, crunched between her mother and father below the table. But half of the pictures looked like art, and half looked like sketches. The difference between the more finished pictures and the rudimentary ones was obvious. He sorted them into two piles with ease. He brought out the drawing Dianne had given him in his office and measured it against the two subsets. He settled it with the finished half.

The finished drawings had contour and shade and range of color. They were well composed and cleanly drawn. They also were very similar. Sophie sat between Dianne and Simon, all three of them under a black table. Mo stood triumphantly above them, with flames all around. After several minutes of studying those, Gordon stacked them and set them aside. The rudimentary set of drawings was what interested Gordon more. Those varied from page to page. In most, Dianne had short hair, but in three, it was long. In one, she was blonde, in the other, brunette. The differences were subtle, but knowing how precious Sophie's colors were to her, Gordon doubted any variance in her drawings was taken lightly. And Simon, to her right, was bald in half of them, his head a horseshoe shape. In the other half, he had long, curly hair. In some, he had a moustache, just a faint line, in others, he had a full beard. The only thing that stayed consistent in those drawings was Sophie and Mo—Sophie a ball of limbs between them and Mo a glorified stick figure, grinning up top.

Gordon found himself drawn to the depictions of Simon. His eyes were covered. If the three of them under the table were like the wise monkeys, Sophie was Hear No Evil—head down, hands scribbled over her ears. Dianne was Speak No Evil—her mouth a thin line throughout, even as the rest of her changed. Simon was See No Evil. His hands often covered his eyes.

In the childish drawings, Simon wore a rich gold wedding ring on his ring finger. In the finished set, his hand was bare, another detail from Sophie's mind that Gordon felt was intentional. Sophie drew her father covering his eyes twenty-five times. *What don't you want your father to see, Sophie?*

Duke had Sophie and Dianne at the moment. Gordon had to wait for things to cool before he approached either of them again, but perhaps Simon could shed some light on the big picture.

Gordon stood back and turned to his mother, who was watching him patiently and seemed to be enjoying herself.

"What are the pictures telling you?" she asked, ever the psychiatrist.

"That perhaps I need to pay a visit to Sophie's dad," Gordon said, and he pulled out his phone. He was about to pull up Marty's phone number but saw that he'd already missed a call from him sometime during his two-hour nodoff. He smiled. He figured that Duke's threats wouldn't be enough to slow Marty down either.

The temporary truce between Marty and him felt tenuous, like soldiers pausing on Christmas day, knowing that in the end, only one of them would be left standing. He knew that when it came to Dana, someone was going to have to back down. Gordon knew it wouldn't be him, but he was sure Marty thought the same.

Still, a truce was a truce, and right then, Gordon needed all the help he could get. So he hit Redial.

Marty picked up on the first ring. "I been tryin' to get a hold of you."

"What do you know about Simon West, Sophie's dad?" Gordon asked.

"Funny you should ask."

CHAPTER ELEVEN

Gordon stood in the valet roundabout of Hopkins until Marty rumbled through in his Charger. Its growl reverberated under the carport, eliciting scowls from the discharged patients and nods of approval from the valet. After Gordon buckled in, Marty pulled out and then promptly in to the gas station across the street. He tapped his hand on the center console between them, palm up and open.

"Twenty bucks," he said. "You put in twenty. I put in twenty."

Gordon felt around in his jacket for his wallet. "Forty bucks for gas? What's this thing get? A mile to the gallon?"

Marty plugged in the spigot and pressed Premium. "Sixteen to the gallon, highway. But Lancaster, PA is an hour and a half away. Maybe your car gets better gas mileage. Maybe it also leaves us stranded on the state line."

Gordon nodded. Marty had a point. While the meter spun on the gas pump outside, Gordon watched the clock on the dash tick inside. Two weeks had passed since Dianne West first called him about Sophie. Four days since

Merryville Prep had first burned. Three days since he'd last spoken to Dana—a dinner he could barely remember attending. How he wished he'd watched her with even half the focus he'd had on Sophie's case that night. What he'd give for one more dinner. He'd ignore everything else but what was right in front of him. *Who* was right in front of him.

Time should have stopped the moment Dana stepped out of it. But time went on. Just about twenty hours were left until his mother stepped out of time herself to remove the cancer in her breast. Two hours after that, she would step back in, God willing.

And one and a half hours to Lancaster, Pennsylvania, where they'd find Simon West and hopefully some answers.

Gordon had no desire to force conversation as they drove, and Marty seemed content focusing on the road. After a time, Gordon closed his eyes, not actually intending to fall asleep. He should have known better.

A loud buzzing awoke him, and he popped his head up with a disconcerting crunch in the neck. He was dreaming of alarms going off in Dana's hospital room, and it took him a good ten seconds to realize that the whining buzz he heard was Marty going over the sleep strips on the highway, wide awake.

"You were drooling on my seats," Marty said.

Gordon wiped at the corner of his mouth and did find a bit of a pool there. He wiped more vigorously, muttering an apology.

Marty ignored it. "I been thinkin' about Sophie," he said and left the words hanging in the car.

"You could have just tapped my shoulder if you wanted to talk," Gordon said, his voice gravelly. "Where are we?"

"Near York. You've been out for like an hour. I think Sophie's got the major in a corner." Marty rattled all that off as if it was related.

Gordon rubbed at a knot in his neck that seemed to have checked in permanently. "Duke? In a corner?"

"Yeah. She's got him pinned in a bad spot. I think he's afraid of her or something. Why else would he be there? Duke doesn't care about anything that doesn't affect his bottom line."

"I don't know," Gordon said skeptically. "He didn't look afraid. You saw the way he talked to her. If we weren't driving to see her dad, I'd say he was scolding her like an angry father."

"I went back to the station to look up the Merryville fire file while you... checked in on Dana." The pause was noticeable but just barely. "You know, to double-check what I'd put in my statement."

"And?"

"And it wasn't there."

"What do you mean it wasn't there?" Gordon adjusted the seatbelt off his collarbone. He felt as though he was losing weight again and bones were showing on him. The new khakis fit almost as badly as the old khakis had, back when he was living on ramen heated in a coffee pot.

"I mean it wasn't there. Not in the paper files. Not on the server. Not anywhere. I know I filed it. I've never misfiled a report in my life."

Gordon was quiet, digesting that most recent puzzle piece.

"I don't misfile," Marty said again, vehemently.

"I'm not saying you did." Gordon held up his hands.

Marty plowed on. "Every case is assigned a lead detective. Every lead detective is assigned to file. Dana..." Marty cleared his throat and focused twice as hard on the pavement in front of him. "Dana gave me this case. Merryville was my first as lead detective. My name was on top of the paperwork. I was the one in charge of the file."

Marty squinched up his mouth for a second. "I didn't misfile it," he said again quietly.

"I believe you. But you know what that means—"

"That means someone deleted it." Marty nodded deeply. "And very few people have admin access to case files. It's a rank thing."

"Rank like major."

"Bingo."

"So you're telling me that there is no record of any suspect in the Merryville fire?" Gordon asked.

"That's what I'm sayin'," Marty said, emphasizing with a thump of his thumb on the steering wheel.

Gordon rested his head back and closed his eyes, picturing Maria tidying up a hospital room that didn't need tidying, that was bare to begin with. "She had no flowers. No cards. Nothing from anybody at the station or anywhere else."

Marty gripped the steering wheel with such force that his shoulders tensed. His eyes hardened under his rock shelf of a brow.

"When I showed up at the station and everybody was going on like nothing happened, I thought they were disrespecting her. I was about to clean house. Then this one guy from the western district that I used to double with sometimes comes up all hushed like, and he asks how Dana's doing recovering from the wreck. He said he'd heard she was in a car wreck. And that booze was involved."

Both men were quiet for a time then, as the Pennsylvania countryside flew by. The October sun had already come full swing into the windshield and the clock had barely struck four. They'd be driving back in the dark.

Simon West lived in a cookie-cutter neighborhood in a suburb on the outskirts of Lancaster, called Centennial. Marty followed his GPS through four-way stop after four-way stop. Gordon could see every house from every other house. The trees were barely higher than the stop signs in most places. Four or five of those trees stacked top to bottom might reach the height of one of the old-growth white oaks of Merryville.

The address Marty had plugged in was coming up on the right: a small ranch house with overgrown fitzer bushes out front covered in fake cobwebs for Halloween. A single string of orange jack-o-lantern lights was hung across half of the front window. Marty parked along the street in front of an unhitched camper covered in fallen leaves, its towline resting on cinder blocks.

Marty shut off the car. "This is it."

"I suppose he knows we're coming."

Marty popped open his door and heaved himself up with one hand on the roof. "Nope. I want to see this guy without him preparing."

"Aren't you supposed to have a warrant?" Gordon crunched his way up the cracked sidewalk behind Marty. "Or some paperwork or something? That says we can be here?"

Marty turned around, and Gordon nearly ran into him.

"We're just talking," Marty said in a way that sounded

as though, if it came down to it, Marty would do nothing of the sort.

A ratty-looking plastic witch by the front door chattered like a set of novelty teeth when the men approached. Marty watched it skeptically as he rang the doorbell. Both men stepped back and waited.

Gordon listened for movement but heard none. So when the door opened suddenly, he couldn't cover his surprised yelp. Even Marty tensed. The man who stood behind the screen door was short and compact, with small, sharp features. He wore a tight-fitted workout shirt, of the type a cyclist would wear, tucked into his jeans. He was muscular in a small, quick way, not unlike Dianne West. He wore a black-and-orange Orioles hat low on his head, with a brim so curved it was almost as if he was surveying them through a spyglass.

"Simon West?" Marty said.

"Who's asking?" he replied, not rudely but straightforward.

"I'm Detective Marty Cicero, with the Baltimore Police." He held up the badge that hung around his neck. "This is Gordon Pope. We were hoping to speak with you."

Gordon fully expected the door to close again. Instead, the man looked closely at them both in a way that Gordon couldn't help but think was quite brazenly childish then nodded rapidly.

"I'm Simon," he said. "I was wondering when you'd come by. Let me guess. This is about my ex-wife."

"Close," Gordon said then paused. No need to play his hand needlessly.

West furrowed his brow for a split second. A small exhale through the nose. "Sophie?" he asked, a shade more quietly.

Gordon nodded. "May we come in, Mr. West?"

West took in a big breath and held it there, pondering. He removed his hat and scratched at his head in thought. He was nearly bald beneath. What hair he had was trimmed neatly to within a centimeter of his head.

"I suppose you should," he said.

Soon, Dana would have to make a choice. She felt it with an undefined sense of foreboding as she sat under the tree in her loop. The foreboding was not unlike the constant, low-level fear that one day, her child would grow up and leave her. One day, her mother would die. One day, she'd realize, as all police do, that the time had come to hang up her shield. She knew she was reaching some final ultimatum on that well-worn path of her brain because the fire starter at the edge of her world was becoming clearer to her.

The part of Dana still tied to the outside world knew how important it was to ID fire starter, knew that people dear to her were tied up intimately with it, including Gordon, whose voice still echoed in the chambers of the loop. She was desperate to see the fire starter as he truly was, and she knew she could. If she made the choice.

But it meant going into the white explosion forever.

Dana didn't know what that meant, not entirely, but she knew it was a final thing. She'd know everything, but it would cost her everything.

So she sat and watched, and the time for her choice neared. The fire starter's face was no longer one she knew, no longer a trick of her mind. It was real. The face taking shape was the one she'd seen in the seconds before the explosion. She'd walked the well-worn path in her brain

long enough to uncover the truth... but he was too far away
to see.

The urge to get closer was almost maddening, like an
itch lodged at the back of her throat that wouldn't go away.
An ID meant a suspect. A suspect led to conviction. A
conviction closed a case. Closing cases was her job.

She found herself on her feet again, behind the static
burn of the fuse, as she had been countless times before. She
walked closer to the fire starter, but that time her walk felt
different. She knew that going into the white that time
meant going away from Chloe and from Gordon forever.

But that itch. She gagged with the persistence of it.
Each step toward the whiteness gave her a tiny reprieve.
That time, the flame of the fuse didn't jump ahead of her. It
waited for her until they were side by side, and it burned
next to her, step by step. Its meaning was clear: *"You can
finally see the truth, but then I take you."*

She almost turned away again to go back to her spot
under the tree, but then she saw how close she was to the
fire starter, how tantalizingly close. Already, she could see
something more, the hat, the ears, clearly delineated,
pushed down at the bill but up at the back—and there, no
hair.

The fire starter was bald.

Still, Dana could only half place him. With every revelation, the urge to move forward grew until it was a hair shy
of unbearable, and she found herself in step with the fuse
again, inches from the cans.

Another tantalizing revelation: the fire starter was not a
child. He was short and trim but not a child. She couldn't
say how old, only that from a distance, his features appeared
childlike when they were not.

With another movement, the fire starter would be hers,

but so would the white. Her choice had come. She started weeping with the pain of indecision.

Then she heard a voice.

"Dr. Pope said I can talk to you as much as I want, and so I will."

Chloe.

"Mr. Buttons walked a long path through the forest every day. And every day, Mr. Buttons tapped the trees with his felt nose so he could find his way back."

Her book. She was reading to Dana. She was... out there.

Dana took a step back. The flame followed, but it flickered and flared as if angry. Dana looked at the fire starter, almost congealed, almost complete, his eyes ever frozen upon her.

"Mr. Buttons was never lost. Until one day, walking through forest frost, he sneezed and found his nose was tossed into a mound of snow."

Her voice danced across the rhymes with confidence. The itch was numbed.

"Help! cried Mr. Buttons as he sat down upon the ground. And he sniffled and he whimpered until he heard a digging sound."

Dana spoke along with her daughter the words she knew by heart: "And up popped Mr. Velvet Mole, who came to him and said: I heard your cry, and here am I, to calm your worried head. I find things for a living. I've really got the knack. Stick with me, and you will see you can find your way back."

"Find your way back."

Chloe's words echoed in her mind until something subtle but definite popped back in place within her. She realized for the first time that she was in a coma. And in that split second of realization, she broke the coma—broke the loop—and slipped upward into a dream where frozen things were no longer frozen.

The fire starter blinked and widened his grin monstrously, all true resemblance gone, until he was a creature made mostly of teeth, with hollow black pits for eyes. After a lifetime of staring at what was essentially a still-life painting peppered here and there with hints of movement, seeing the fire starter break free of his frozen position and turn fully toward her made her scream out in silence.

Dana turned and ran, and the fire starter followed. She heard the susurrant scampering of tiny feet behind her, like the sound of a cockroach dashing on kitchen tile. The two of them were in a footrace once again.

Dana ran to the edge of her world. She felt fingers of fire reach for her, their heat searing her back. She flung herself off the edge of her mind, and she fell.

DANA FRISCO WOKE UP, not with a shout or a jolt—she was too stiff for that—but with a single squeeze of Chloe's hand in hers.

Her daughter met her eyes, dropped her book, and threw herself on top of her mother, tubes and attachments and bandages be damned, until Dana's mother pulled her away. At first, she scolded Chloe. Then her eyes met Dana's, and her tears joined Chloe's as she fell to her knees.

Movement was agony for Dana, but she could do it. She wiggled her toes and squeezed her daughter's hand again and again. She felt a terrible blockage in her throat and realized it was a ventilator. She fought off panic as the room screamed with alarms. She scrabbled weakly at the mask and might have attempted to rip the tube from her throat herself if Chloe's hand hadn't kept her still while the crash cart came in. The staff was clearly expecting to see a dying woman, and the doctor in the lead nearly dropped the defibrillator paddles when he saw her looking back at him. She waited for another eternity while they tended to her, pulling things from her with sickening pressure on the inside and outside, where no pressure should ever be felt.

All she wanted to do was work moisture into her mouth. All she wanted to do was tell Gordon what she knew to be true about the fire starter, what she'd seen before the coma broke.

She prayed she wasn't too late.

MORE FAKE COBWEBS festooned the banister just inside the house of Simon West. An empty plastic bowl sat on a small end table offset from the base of the stairs, awaiting candy. A plastic skull grinned beside it with fake tea-light candles that glowed orange inside its eye sockets. West walked ahead of them under a line of plastic bats hanging from plastic strings.

"Watch the bats. They get tangled," he said, not looking back. Both men ducked under.

"You're pretty into Halloween, Mr. West?" Marty asked.

"You have to be, with a ten-year-old. It's a prime Halloween age. Sophie never much cared for it." West gestured at a plastic tarpaulin with two dancing skeletons taped to the patio door. "I suspect she had enough of all this in her own mind. But Dustin's different. Loves all the ghoulish stuff. Can I get you men something to drink? Water? I think I might have a beer somewhere in the back of the fridge." Simon spoke in flat monotone, and quickly, as if his mind was a sentence or two ahead of his mouth.

"We're fine, thanks," Gordon said.

West paused briefly and nodded then sat down at the table, gesturing at the chairs. "So what did Sophie do?"

"Not so much Sophie, Mr. West. It's her friend. Mo."

West held Gordon's gaze without blinking. "Her imaginary friend. Yes. She's caused quite a bit of trouble with her imaginary friend. Don't tell me she's starting fires again."

"She's not. As a matter of fact, I don't believe she ever was," Gordon said, leaning forward and crossing his arms on the small dinner table. "But Mo was. Because Mo is real. And Mo has been real for a long time. We saw him ourselves, on the deck of 8 Long Lane."

West still hadn't blinked. Gordon felt as if he was in a chess match with the man. The opening move was when he'd invited them in. Gordon was struck by how little surprise the man showed. It said something without saying anything at all. It said that West knew—in some form, at least. He knew that Mo was real. And he was keeping it to himself.

Marty was unabashedly casing the house. He craned his neck to see around West to the far wall, where family pictures hung in a neat row. In one, Simon West stood with his second wife, a kind-looking young woman in a conservative dress with green eyes framed by herringbone eyeglasses. Their son Dustin sat between them, lodged comfortably between the pockets of their shoulders.

"I can just bring the photo over to you, Detective. If you want to know what Dustin looks like."

Simon seemed oddly at ease with two strangers in his house—one of them a cop snooping around his family—almost as if he'd been preparing for that day. He stood and walked to the pictures, and as he panned them, Gordon caught a half smile, as if even then West was reliving those moments. He plucked the largest from the wall, a framed portrait the size of a sheet of paper of the three of them outside a carnival game, the kind where you shoot a squirt gun in a hole to fill up a balloon until it pops.

"My wife, Sally, and our son. This was taken six months ago."

Gordon saw Marty's face fall as he looked at the picture. Marty had hoped to find their fire starter, but the child in the picture was in a wheelchair. When Gordon looked up again, he found West watching him carefully.

"Dustin has a mild form of cystic fibrosis. It occasionally happens with high-risk pregnancies. Sally was forty-two when we had him. As you can see, my son isn't the type to light fires and run away."

His eyes showed no triumph, and his tone was assured but not gloating. If he felt he'd caught both men out, he wasn't showing it.

"You were granted no custody over Sophie at all?" Gordon asked.

"On paper, I have limited custody. If Dianne were to bring Sophie here, I could watch her, be her father again. Dianne has not. So I haven't. Dustin and his half sister are strangers. They've seen each other perhaps three times in their lives. I wanted it otherwise, of course, but the custody battle saw to that."

Gordon had been involved in more than his fair share of custody battles. When he was first starting out, he had seen many patients with parents spiraling quickly toward divorce. He often was called in to testify on behalf of a child in court. Gordon prided himself on being able to tell very quickly where best care lay. He'd seen firsthand what

Dianne West did with her time, and while Simon West set him ill at ease, the impression he gave wasn't any worse than what he got from Dianne.

"Seems strange to me that you wouldn't be granted any custody at all," Gordon said.

"It does, doesn't it?" West replied. "Dianne is a drinker. Dianne dabbled in pills. Just sleep medication, at first. But I knew she was going harder when I wasn't looking. On paper, it's a no-brainer to give custody to me."

"On paper," Gordon said, waiting.

"In reality, there's Warren Duke." West looked at both of them as if they had known all along. When they remained silent, he furrowed his brow, but only slightly. "You do know about Warren's involvement, don't you? I assumed so, given that you're police."

Marty turned slightly to Gordon, met his gaze briefly, and shrugged. Gordon nodded. He was as tired of charades as Marty. They could play Battleship in the dark or try to get to the bottom of things. Time was running out for every player on the board.

"We know Warren Duke is involved. He was at the house on Long Lane the night we saw Mo. But in all honesty, we have no idea why. We were hoping you might shed some light on that."

West smiled grimly and sat back in his chair. "I don't know who you think you saw on that veranda, but I can tell you this: I'd stay out of it. Sophie could set half the city on fire with Mo dancing behind her the whole way, and she'd still never see the inside of a mental-health facility. Warren Duke wouldn't allow such a dark mark on the family name."

Gordon slumped. The puzzle piece fit, but it darkened the picture as a whole. "The family. Of course."

"Warren Duke is Sophie's uncle. Before Dianne was Dianne West, she was Dianne Duke."

West kept speaking while Gordon's mind reeled. So Warren Duke was in the family. He was protecting the family name or, as was more likely, the upward trend of his career. After major came deputy director then director—all positions that were highly vetted and extremely political. Who actually had set fire to school—whether it was Mo or Sophie—didn't matter as much as how it looked. And it looked as though Sophie had set the fires. Committing her would all but confirm her guilt. Men had lost appointments to deputy director for far less.

"His relationship to Dianne, and to Sophie, isn't something he speaks of," Simon continued. "He's quite guarded about it. Fiercely so. He was as thrilled as I've seen him when the divorce was finalized and I moved out here. He thinks Sophie's mental troubles come from my side of the family."

"Do you agree with him?" Gordon asked. "I mean, have you ever been evaluated, or anyone on your side..."

"No. I refuse even to brook the argument. Not from Dianne, not from either of you, but especially not from Warren." He spoke with an abrupt ferocity before calming himself visibly with a deep breath. The silence around his exhalation was palpable. West tapped the table lightly with his knuckles. "And now, if you men will excuse me, I have a dinner to make before Sally gets home with Dustin."

Gordon knew they had no precedent to stay longer. He stood first. Marty followed, slowly, none too happy. Gordon could tell Marty didn't like Simon West and didn't trust him one bit. He knew that flinty look well enough. Marty often looked at Gordon that way.

They walked silently to the door. The sun was on the far

side of the day already, and the temperature was dipping quickly, the first freeze of the year just around the corner. As Gordon buttoned his jacket, and before West could close the door behind him, he decided to throw caution to the wind.

"Can I ask you why you and Dianne separated? Or was that because of Duke too?"

"Warren's reach is long, but not that long," West replied flatly. "Dianne's an addict. I didn't want to spend my life picking up after her. Although neither side was too hurt to say goodbye. That's how you know. When it ends without much of a bang, you realize it never had any power behind it in the first place."

"Why does she do that to herself? The pills, the booze?"

"For that, I think you'll have to ask her."

Gordon nodded and turned around again, but Simon spoke up once more.

"Try not to hold it against her. Suffice to say that she had a hard time watching Sophie grow up. A hard time letting go. That house was meant for a huge family. Soon, it will just be her."

GORDON WAS LOST in his own thoughts as Marty drove them back to Baltimore. An expectant quiet gathered in the car as both men tried to make sense of what they'd learned.

They were nearing the halfway point when Marty muttered, "Do you think it was him?" His voice was so low that Gordon almost missed it.

"Him? You mean Simon?"

"Do you think it was him that started the fires?"

Gordon pondered the thought. If he was honest with himself, he was trying harder to fit Warren Duke into the role of fire starter than Simon West. Duke would never touch the match himself, of course—he'd have some paid thug to do that... but no. As much as Gordon wanted to paint Duke the villain, he knew the man was trying to shove Sophie under the rug, not bring her out into the light by drawing attention to the family with flame.

"I don't know," he answered. "Could be, I suppose."

"He has the build. Think about it. We've been thinking all along it's a kid Sophie's age, but none of us saw him up close. Maybe Mo is man. A small man."

Gordon pictured Mo in his mind. Manic grin. Hands on hips. Finger to his lips. *"Shhh."*

Marty gripped the steering wheel with both hands as if he wanted to rip it from the dash. The car accelerated, ripping down the highway as Marty opened up.

"I mean, think about it, right? Dude gets shut out of his kid's life? Has a grudge against his wife's family? Maybe the only way he can see his daughter is by following her around like her imaginary friend, raising hell for his ex-wife as he goes."

Gordon was pressed gently back in his seat again. He checked his seat belt was fastened with a quick touch and settled it flat across his chest.

"It fits, yeah," Gordon said, "but why tell us all that, then? I mean, why let us in at all? To gloat?"

Marty didn't slow down at the city limits, only switched lanes more aggressively, lost in thought. Gordon didn't dare speak to him. Any break in Marty's concentration might end up breaking them both in two.

They were just past the 695 interchange when Gordon got a text. He pulled his phone from his pocket and read it before looking at the sender:

Am awake. Can't speak. Slowly putting myself together. They will allow visitors in three hours.

It was from Dana.

Gordon forgot all about how fast they were going, forgot all about Simon West. All thoughts about Dianne and Sophie were blown from his mind. He braced himself with one hand on Marty's massive shoulder and whooped until Marty was forced to slow.

"It's from her! She's awake! She's awake, man! We can see her later tonight!"

Marty's mood broke. A smile cracked his face like a single ray of sunshine beaming through a thunderhead. "Thank Christ," he said.

Dana sent a second text quickly afterward: *Fire starter is old. Adult. And bald.*

Gordon's silence piqued Marty, who asked, "What is it? What's wrong?"

Gordon read him the text hesitantly. Marty's face fell. Gordon knew what he was thinking. Simon West was old. And Simon West was bald. They'd seen it when he removed his hat briefly.

"I knew it," Marty said, deadly calm.

"Now, just hold on a second. Let's try to make sense of this."

Marty shook his head, gripped the wheel tighter, and made a nearly suicidal exit, scattering debris across the median and nearly running a camper off the road.

"I'm going back," Marty said, reading the signs for directions back to 83 North. He was approaching a stoplight at an alarming speed.

"What are you gonna do? Just drag him out of his house?"

"That's probable cause in my book," Marty said, ticking

his head toward Gordon's phone, still in his hands. "Shouldn't have a problem at the station, not for a man within a hairsbreadth of being a cop killer."

"Nobody at the station *knows anything*, Marty. We'll see her in a couple of hours, and we can clear all this up." Gordon tried to talk him down like one of his patients, but that only seemed to rile him further.

"Oh, I'll see her, all right. With a nice present. Simon West in cuffs."

Gordon saw a way out. The signs ahead were for Towson. Merryville was just past Towson, perhaps ten minutes away.

"There's another way. Let's go to Long Lane. We can confront Dianne directly about Simon *and* Duke. Maybe get a warrant."

Marty said, "There's another reason people talk so freely like Simon did. It's 'cause they think they can't get caught. You go talk to Dianne if you want. It didn't get us far last time, and it won't this time. I'm going to talk to Simon West."

So IT WAS that Gordon found himself in front of the Merryville gate once more. The leaves on the iron seemed to have turned bloodred just in the past forty-eight hours. The deep-earth rumble of Marty's Charger faded in the distance as the quiet, bespectacled attendant stood and set his battered paperback down spine up, waiting patiently while Gordon approached.

"Dr. Gordon Pope, here for Sophie West."

Gordon prayed he had a standing invitation as the attendant scanned a list on his clipboard with a single finger. The man nodded, and Gordon did his best not to sag with relief. "I suppose you know the way by now, Doctor?"

"I do."

The gate swung open, and Gordon walked in.

AFTER TEXTING GORDON, Dana was hit with a wave of exhaustion. What mattered next was recovering, finding full movement again, regaining normal speech. The face of the fire starter was already fading, in the way that dreams do. The revelation that he was not a child at all, that he was suffering, himself—those things seemed to matter less and less by the moment as she hugged her daughter and was held by her mother and worked her swollen tongue into shape once again. The worry and fear that gripped her upon first opening her eyes faded. Soon Gordon would be with her, and Marty as well. Together, they could tackle the case in good time. The realness of the world around her was what mattered—the true and changing light and sound and feel of the place she had awoken into once more, along with the solid presence of her daughter by her side.

Then Deborah Pope was at her door, and she was smiling warmly, if a little sadly. Dana was confused. Deborah could not possibly have known she was awake yet. And Deborah looked terrible. She was drained and weak, standing only with the help of a harried-looking attendant. Then she noticed the loose gown and the plastic bracelet, and she knew. She knew immediately that something was eating Deborah Pope from the inside. Only cancer could bring a woman like her to such a state.

In her hand, she held a stack of papers.

"Hello, sweetheart," she said, with a fondness that

brought tears to Dana's eyes. "He'll be so happy to see you." She glanced behind her at the staff accompaniment, who tapped his watch. "I wish I could be there for the reunion. But I have no time left. The surgery team is already assembled. So it's up to you to tell him." She held up the papers. "He rushed off looking for the wrong person and left these with me. I've been studying them for some time. There is a pattern to these drawings, a very sad one, and I think my son has put himself in a great deal more danger than even he knows."

CHAPTER TWELVE

L ong Lane was silent. No cars passed Gordon as he walked. The street and sidewalks were cold and hard and clean, as if every leaf that fell from the dwindling canopy above was snatched in the air before it even hit the ground. Hedges and solid brick fences loomed to his right and left, blotting out what little light there was from the houses themselves.

He wondered if perhaps he should have gone with Marty after all. Then he heard the quiet click of the gate closing shut behind him, and he knew his decision was made. He pictured Sophie walking back from school in the dark like that, a troubled girl trapped in her own head, worrying about things no child her age should worry about, so secluded from the world that she became terrified of what lay beyond the walls of her own neighborhood. And when her condition gave voice to her fears, she felt she had no choice but to burn everything clean again. Like cauterizing a wound.

She couldn't bring herself to start the fires, but she'd found someone who could, someone who turned her psychosis into reality, who knew her sickness as deeply as she did herself, and who was unafraid to light it up. Someone older. Someone balding. Possibly Simon West, although Gordon wasn't as sure as Marty. West was off, true, and strangely intense, but he was also guarded and private. He didn't strike Gordon as the type of person to stand grinning over his work like Mo, hands on hips. Mo smiled every time anyone had seen him—unrelentingly, almost as if he was stricken with rictus. Simon West hadn't smiled once.

Their biggest problem was that if Simon West *wasn't* Mo, they were back to square one with no more leads.

Gordon came upon 8 Long Lane, rounding the soft bend of the street until the whitewashed-wood-and-brick façade came into view. The house was stunning in the sunset, well-kept and proud. Any passerby would have no idea how empty it was inside. He hoped that at least one of the two inhabitants had the wherewithal to answer his questions.

The wide-open front door and darkened anteroom suggested otherwise. *For a family so concerned with their secrets, they sure don't care for locks.* Or, as was more likely, Sophie was wandering again.

As he approached, he couldn't help but remember that all the previous times he'd come, the door had been closed—unlocked but closed. That it hung open seemed more like an invitation. The door might have been wide open for some time—hours, perhaps most of the day, waiting for him.

Gordon pulled out his cell phone and thought to call someone. Anyone. But he had nobody to call. At the threshold before the darkness, he was struck for the first time with the reality that his mother was now in prep for surgery. The enormity of that hit him like a surge of cold water in the open ocean, and he found himself leaning against the doorpost. She'd made him promise to stay away, but it still felt like a betrayal. He could call, but she was beyond picking up.

Might never pick up again.

He shook that dread thought away. He could call Dana, but she wouldn't answer either. She was going through the long, aching process of coming back into the world. A body paused doesn't easily start again. She couldn't even speak.

So he was alone. Still, he refused to enter without some note of his passing, so he texted Dana.

Marty went to follow a lead in Lancaster. I'm asking questions at 8 Long Lane.

He sent it, stared at his phone, and typed again.

I think I need more friends.

Sent that, too.

I miss you terribly. Can't wait to hold you again.

Sent.

Gordon took a deep breath and told himself to put away the phone. He sometimes got that way. He had with his ex-wife. He didn't need to start with his girlfriend as well. He pocketed the phone and took a step inside.

The marbled flooring of the foyer seemed electric with the moonlight that cut through the large slot windows above the front door. Gordon hardly spared a glance to his right or left as he walked through to the great room. He was sure he would find nothing out back tonight, either. If they were around, Dianne and Sophie would be upstairs, where he already heard the tinny, frantic buzz of the television on low volume. The great room was so dim that Gordon could see the television's light from where he stood on the floor below —flashes of white that crept around the open double doors leading to Dianne's bedroom.

Gordon called their names as loudly as he could, in part so his voice might rouse one or both of them, and in part to dispel the strange dread that drifted over the place like low-lying mist.

"Mo?" he added.

Nothing. Gordon walked to the stairs, pushing forward one step at a time, all the way up. He decided against further calling and instead listened, trying to hear the tell-tale patter of feet or the quiet moaning of Sophie hidden away somewhere, but all was quiet.

Gordon expected something awful when he turned the corner to see the bed. He wasn't sure what—a grinning man-child, perhaps, or a book of matches in a speckled swath of blood where Dianne should be. Instead, he found Dianne again, eyes closed, breathing deeply. One arm was flung wistfully over her forehead, the other draped partly off the bed, her covers strewn.

Gordon was almost disappointed. He looked for the pills briefly but couldn't find them on the dresser or in it. He smelled the full glass and pitcher on the nightstand to her left. Water. No vodka bottles to be seen. Gordon thought that odd, but perhaps she'd medicated downstairs, watching the darkened playhouse out back, and only made her way up when the world was comfortably numb again and she could collapse into sleep.

A second source of light shone electric blue from the corner, her computer. It was awake, which was also odd. Gordon put off the awkward decision of how best to rouse Dianne and instead walked to the desk and sat in the small chair there, still warm. He looked back at Dianne. She must have only recently passed out, which was good because she would be easier to rouse.

So this was the book—Dianne's memoir, the magnum

opus she sometimes seemed to care more about than her own daughter. At first blush, it looked like Dianne had been suffering some sort of odd writer's block. The page was black with words, paragraph after paragraph, but each was simply a repetition of one word, a name. The first was *Sophie*, repeated two hundred or so times. The next paragraph was her own name, *Dianne*, repeated another two hundred times, maybe more.

Another break. Another name. *Ashley*. Again and again. Then *Peter* followed by *Sarah* and *Andrew*. Each their own block of text.

After Andrew came *MOMOMOMOMOMOMOMO*. No breaks. At first, Gordon thought Dianne had written *Mom*, but as he scrolled, it dawned on him that she had written *Mo* for almost twenty pages. Gordon ended up scrolling faster and faster and thought perhaps all of the document—all four hundred pages of it—was *Mo*, but at page seventy-five, it started over again with Sophie. Then Dianne. Ashley. Peter. Sarah. Andrew.

MOMOMOMOMOMOMOMOMOMOMOMO
MOMOMOMOMOMOMOMOMOMOMOMO
MOMOMOMOMOMOMOMOMOMOMOMO
MOMOMOMOMOMOMOMOMOMOMOMO

Gordon's breathing quickened. He'd found the right piece of the puzzle at last.

A rustling and a creak came from the bed. Gordon turned and found Dianne sitting up stock still, with her hair over her face. He was too startled to react, sitting in her desk chair, one elbow up on its back, watching her with blank horror, as if a foul ball had been careened off right at his face and he was powerless to duck.

"Dianne?" Gordon whispered because he was no longer so sure.

Her bobbed blond hair hung over the front of her face, backward and askew, like a poorly groomed show dog, but it had to be Dianne. Her trim arms and sharp fingers reached up and parted the hair in front of her face, and beneath it was a grinning set of white teeth and manic, swimming eyes —eyes that were Dianne's but also were not.

With one hand, Dianne pulled off her wig, and beneath it was a patchy, scabbed mess. Her head was shaved to bleeding across the front and tufted in the back, where it looked as though clumps of it had been pulled out by her own hand. She grabbed the crystal pitcher, her fingers snaking around the handle with a solid grip. Gordon saw it happening but couldn't take his eyes off her face.

There it was, the black hole in the picture where his puzzle piece fit. Gordon was looking at Dianne, but he was seeing Mo. He waited for it to make sense, for his brain to catch up with himself, but it didn't. He felt no satisfaction in finishing the puzzle just to find the picture a jumbled horror show.

In the time it took for Gordon to stand up, Mo had sprung to his feet and flung the crystal pitcher with surprising speed and accuracy at Gordon's head. A glittering arc of water left the pitcher as if jet propelled, and he thought it was quite beautiful, spinning slowly, like a constellation of stars.

He felt the water hit him first, just a few splashes, like rain on his face. Then the pitcher connected solidly with the side of Gordon's head, and everything went black.

Marty Cicero was already halfway to Lancaster, teeth gritted, knuckles white on the steering wheel. He drove in near silence, his mind on Simon West but also on Dana. He ran scenarios through his head, of how grateful she'd be when he could show up with the case closed. The man who'd put a piece of metal in her head would be safely behind six inches of solid metal himself, for the rest of his life. She might even smile that stunner of a smile, made all the more powerful on account of how rare it was. He hoped she could still smile. The blast had spared her face, so there was a good chance. Almost cost her an arm, but they could work through that together. Rehab it. Get her back in fighting shape. More than anything, he wanted to make her smile again.

The buzz of his phone in the cup holder jarred him back to the road and the speed he was going—damn near 105. He had to get his driving under control. He hadn't meant to let Pope see him like that. The only place he could blow off steam was in his car, and he took advantage, but from the way Pope triple-checked his seat belt, Marty was pretty sure the man was never getting in his car again.

Fine. He'd never asked for Pope's help. Never once. Didn't need to.

He snatched the phone up and looked at it and saw *Dana Frisco* on the caller ID and involuntarily hit the brakes so that he fishtailed a little before he could get himself under control. His face was flushed, and his mouth went dry.

"Dana?"

Her voice was scratchy, as if she was speaking through an old radio, but it was her. "Marty, listen. Mo is Dianne. Dianne West. Do you hear me? Where are you? Please tell me you're with Gordon. I can't get a hold of him."

"I'm..." Marty blinked. The flush that hit his face crept down his neck. From nervous to embarrassed in an instant—and when Marty Cicero was embarrassed, he got mad to cover it up.

"Well, it's nice to hear from you too, partner. You know I've been doing nothing but worry myself sick over you for the past three days?"

"He's not picking up his phone," Dana said, plowing forward as if Marty hadn't spoken at all. That, more than her words, made it eminently clear to him where her heart lay. He felt as if someone had just landed a blow to his sternum.

Marty swallowed hard, forcing his head to clear and becoming a cop again. "I left him in Merryville to follow up a lead," he said, and perhaps the frost that flattened his voice gave Dana pause, or perhaps she was dreading the answer he'd given, because she was silent on the other end of the line. "It was a good lead—"

"Marty, listen to me. You've got to get back there now. She'll kill him. She thinks... It doesn't matter what she thinks. All that matters for you is that you get there and get him out." She was already losing her voice. She sounded exhausted. "I'm gonna call it in now, send the squad if I can, but Duke might interfere. I know he's involved in this. So it's probably gonna be up to you."

"Dana..."

"Save him, Marty," she said, her voice a pleading whisper. "Please. Don't let him die."

She trailed off and hung up. Marty dropped his phone into the cup holder in the console. He did not stop. He did not turn around. Marty continued on like that for another three miles, listening to the engine. Part of him contemplated continuing on forever, ripping up the road ahead and never looking back, but he couldn't outrun what he felt for Dana, just as surely as Dana couldn't hide what she felt for Gordon.

What eventually got to Marty—what made him slam his open palms against the steering wheel and take risky advantage of a half-paved emergency access road to flip around and gun it back the way he'd come—wasn't actually Dana. It was Gordon and the picture Marty had in his mind of Gordon coming out from the library, Warren Duke's gun in his face. Gordon Pope had subtly waved him off, kept him hidden, and saved his job. Gordon had done all that for him despite knowing damn well that Marty Cicero did not like him and probably never would.

Gordon was a huge liability from a professional standpoint for both Marty and Dana. He'd stolen away from Marty any chance at a different life with Dana—a life of love returned—but he was also a good man. And good men deserved help if they needed it.

Marty squealed into the far-left lane, thick tires spinning. He floored it again, muttering every filthy word he could muster from years as a cop and decades of living through everything Baltimore had thrown at him before that. When the muttering didn't make him feel any better, he roared right along with the engine.

GORDON WATCHED his mother on the operating table. He stood in an observation room of some sort, separated from the doctors by glass. They moved around her like wraiths with steel teeth flashing as they cut. Gordon pressed against the glass to see as best he could, but his mother was shrouded in a blur of blue-clad men and women in white masks. He pressed harder and harder, and the side of his face ached terribly with the pressure, burned with it. The sea of blue and white parted for a moment, and he saw his mother staring right at him even as they cut her with terrible tugging motions. The steady, unblinking force of her gaze staggered him back from the glass, but the awful burning pain remained. Her mouth opened, and she spoke his name in silence. Gordon couldn't respond, but to his right, he heard a soft, subtle creaking sound that struck him as terribly familiar, like a woman sitting up in a bed, and when he turned to look, he found Dianne, head shaved, scabbed, tufted, and bleeding. He almost screamed until he realized she was paying him no mind. She was reaching out to the operating room with the same yearning as Gordon had before, and when Gordon followed her grasping hand, he saw that his mother had been swapped out. Now, Sophie lay on the operating table.

"*Sophie*," Dianne croaked. "*Ashley. Peter. Sarah. Andrew—*"

Dianne burned. She went up in flames without the cry of *Mo* on her lips. Gordon could smell it. The char was overpowering...

GORDON COUGHED himself awake and immediately regretted it. He felt each hack tap on his brain like an icepick. Jagged explosions the color of rust and blood erupted behind his closed eyes. He grabbed at the nucleus of his pain and immediately regretted it again. His hand came away wet with blood. He couldn't see it, but he felt it.

He couldn't see much of anything. At first, he thought that he'd gone blind, that someone had stolen away his sight before leaving him on a hard floor in a hot room filled with smoke, but as his eyes adjusted, a crack of white light mate-rialized before him. Gordon pawed at it and found slatted wood. The wood gave, and the crack of light grew. He kicked out at it, and the wood gave completely. A door. He was in a closet. As it swung open, a wave of smoke poured in, and Gordon reeled, nearly vomiting. He covered his nose with the crook of his arm, squinted his eyes against the burn, and scooted out of the very same linen closet that Marty Cicero had concealed himself within a day earlier.

Out of the hazy darkness, he emerged into a raging inferno. Arms of reaching flames spread from Dianne's bedroom, belching gouts of smoke that billowed upward and piled upon the ceiling like a deadly thunderhead around the chandelier.

More smoke poured in a thick and steady stream from the library across the hall, and a loud crackling sound told Gordon the books were going up in flames. Gordon grabbed a silk fitted sheet and draped himself in it then scampered by the fire in the bedroom. If Dianne was in there, she was a goner, but Gordon doubted she was. She was Mo, after all, and Mo never got caught in his flames.

What worried Gordon was that Sophie was still unac-counted for. The events leading up to the attack all fell into place, and Gordon despaired to find she had no part in them. The fires would likely trigger an attack. If she was already in a manic state, they stood a good chance of elevating her to a catatonic state. She could be paralyzed somewhere.

He tried to check the library. The flames hadn't yet reached the door, but the closer he came, the more intense was the heat, and he had to turn away. He looked beyond the linen closet to where her bedroom would be, but as he did, a crack resounded as a ball of fire erupted from Dianne's room, expanding out to char the hallway. If she was anywhere on the second floor, she was gone. And if Gordon didn't get out soon, he'd be gone too.

He ran for the stairs, and there he saw a jagged swath of color, as if someone had dragged a fistful of colored pencils against the pristine white wallpaper leading down the stairs. It was unmistakable. On purpose. A sign that said, "Follow me."

Gordon needed no convincing.

The rainbow trailed downstairs, jumped the banister, and picked up again on the floor of the great room behind the buffalo. From there, Gordon hoped it might go out the front door into a crisp autumn night, but it didn't. It went behind the great room toward the kitchen.

Gordon paused at the front door. He had a chance to get away and stay alive. He could stand at the perimeter and watch the house get consumed, praying that Sophie and Dianne had somehow gotten out.

The problem was Gordon didn't believe that they had. He believed the rainbow mark was more than a trail—it was a cry for help. At the end of it, he would find Sophie. If he hurried, he could get her out alive.

He turned from the door and followed the rainbow deeper into the house. The fires were upstairs, but they wouldn't be for long. Already, the smoke was muddying the light on the main floor. The chandelier above looked like a foggy lighthouse seen from a distance. Gordon followed the lines of colored pencil with his fingers as well as his eyes. Sophie had dug deep into the felted wallpaper, ripping it as she went. The rainbow wrapped the backstop of the great room, and for a moment, Gordon thought he'd lost the trail. He spun in a slow circle in a near panic, and he froze when he saw what looked like an enormous orange slug crawling out of the stove.

He squinted through the smoke until he recognized the lace curtains from the back door, the ones that had billowed in the wind what felt like a lifetime before. They were bundled blobs of flame, dragged from their hangers and jammed into the oven, set to broil. He ran toward them with a mind to pull the sink sprayer out, but when he was feet away, they went up with a *whoomp* he could feel in his gut. He staggered backward. No more distractions. *Follow the rainbow, follow the rainbow, follow the rainbow.*

Coming back from the kitchen, he was able to spot the rainbow again—on the whitewashed walls leading downstairs.

"Stupid, stupid, stupid," Gordon muttered as he rattled down the stairs, barely touching each, burying himself deeper in the flaming house.

He came upon the main basement, which looked finished and pristine, with a massive projection television and several rows of plush leather viewing chairs, but the rainbow didn't stop there. It went deeper, and Gordon followed until he found himself another floor down, in a large unfinished cellar. The front half was entirely taken up by rack upon rack of wine. The light from the hall died ten feet in. The smoke hadn't found its way there yet, but Gordon knew it was coming. Already, he was sweating profusely. His shirt was drenched, and his brow was wet. He wiped down the front of his face and reset his glasses, but that was like turning on the wipers in a downpour. He couldn't keep up.

"Sophie! It's Gordon!"

The roar of the fire was muted there, replaced by an eerie hissing and a subtle moan—not of a frightened little girl but of cool air escaping out around his legs. On the floor far above, something heavy fell with a reverberating boom. Time was very, very short.

He flicked the light switch several times, to no avail. He pushed through his fear and walked deeper into the cellar, looking for the rainbow, but the rainbow had stopped. When he reached the first row of bottles, he found a handful of colored pencils scattered on a small table, next to a solitary glass of wine, a cigar box full of corks, and a small penlight.

Gordon clicked the penlight on. It would have been perfect for a better look at the labels deep in the collection, had the house not been on its way to collapsing around him in a blazing inferno. The light did little aside from illuminate what was right in front of his face, and what he saw was smoke. He coughed violently, as if in the seeing he finally believed. He figured he had five minutes to get up to the basement proper and find a recessed window to climb out of. He'd seen one when he was rolling around on the lawn a lifetime ago. Not much time, but five minutes was still five minutes. He had a chance to find her.

He noticed that while the bottles were mostly caked in dust, one row of wine looked as though fingers had brushed a swath along a line that led deeper into the cellar. He hunched over and followed it, blind to everything else. Soon he was quite far back. He guessed the collection had well over a thousand bottles, untouched for years, except for that brush of a hand. It bounced over each in turn... until Gordon reached the end.

The wine rack went on, but the wine stopped. He guessed he was near the back wall, although he couldn't be sure. That eerie hissing was louder, the air less smoky but thickening by the minute.

"Sophie?"

No answer. Gordon stood on his tiptoes to look over the racks, but he was just a hair short. He crouched down, peered between the racks, and saw that the collection hadn't really stopped, that in fact at least one more bottle was jammed farther back in the rack, almost out of sight. He reached in and felt for it, but what he pulled out wasn't a wine bottle. It was a mason jar, small, half the standard size and filled a quarter way with red liquid. He turned it slowly until he found a piece of paper tape on its back side. On the tape was the name "Andrew."

Part of Gordon understood what he was seeing because his hand started to shake slightly. The reverence with which he returned it to its spot indicated that his body, at least, understood, even if his mind was running behind.

He moved down the line and shone the light into the next slot. There he found another jar the same size, and he pulled it out and turned it over, an inch of liquid rolling viscously inside. On its lid was another piece of tape that read "Sarah."

Gordon cocked his head as if he still didn't understand, but he was lying to himself. His body betrayed him further —his hand trembled fully. The jar clacked softly upon the wood as he replaced it.

Gordon moved mechanically to the next slot. He could do nothing else... until he saw another jar. A large jar.

The fire and smoke were pushed to the back of his mind, but they were very much at the front of his senses. The acrid, overpowering forest-fire scent of roasting stone and sizzling wood had been turning his stomach without his knowing. Seeing that jar brought the pique to full. His mouth filled with spittle, and his stomach surged, but he fought it down. He refused to vomit. He felt it would be disrespectful to the jars, to what they held.

The large jar was the size of a flower vase. It was marked "Peter" and "Sarah" on two separate pieces of dry, yellowed tape. In the smoky haze of the penlight, he saw two very small floating figures within a sea of red, barely defined, more like clumps of twisted sticks than anything recognizable. But Gordon knew. He turned away, fell away, pushed himself back against the far wall. He was in shock less because of what he'd seen and more because of how he'd missed seeing it all along. He only stopped dragging himself against the concrete when his backside slammed squarely into a workbench set flush in the most distant corner of the house.

He turned to feel his way around it, shining the penlight in vain. All he could see was a slow, sinister roiling of smoke in the shallow cone of its light. The tabletop was made of stone and still quite cold. He had no idea how big it was and tried to walk around it. He took in a big breath to call out for Sophie again but ended up with a lungful of smoke. He coughed violently, his head splitting again, sickly orange stars everywhere.

A hand shot out from the blackness and grabbed him around an ankle. Gordon would have screamed if he wasn't coughing. Instead, he braced himself on the cold black table and dipped low, ready to grab hold of whatever was grabbing hold of him.

He grabbed Sophie. Even though he couldn't see her face, he recognized her plaid uniform. He collapsed to sitting, coughing still. He felt as if he was trying to breathe while buffeted by waves. Perhaps one in five breaths actually got where it was supposed to. The rest were blown right back out.

What eventually stilled him was the look on Sophie's face as she shot out from the darkness, inches from his nose, with a single finger over her lips. *"Shhh."*

Her face was manic, eyes wider than was natural, in snakelike focus. She didn't blink, despite the smoke, her mouth open slightly. She looked pained, as though it took an enormous amount of initiative just to move, much less grab hold of Gordon. She leaned back against the concrete wall beneath the black table and looked forward again as if Gordon wasn't there. He leaned back too. The concrete was blissfully cold, the kind of cold that made him desperate to dive into snow or stand under a hose or sink deep into a lake.

His shoes slipped on what Gordon thought were scraps of paper, rolled scrolls, but as he slapped at one, his hand stuck to it. He peeled it off and brought it to his face and saw he was holding a sheet of uncut photographs, one of many that lay scattered around them. They looked like pictures of a grainy eclipse, but Gordon recognized them as ultrasound prints. They were dated twelve years before and clearly marked with pen on top:

West, Dianne M.
Day 78.

Two granulated blobs were circled. Twins. Over the left fetus, the word *Sophie?* was handwritten in cheerful script. Over the right was a smiley face and a series of excited question marks and exclamation marks.

Sophie's twin. Gordon set his tired head back against the concrete and closed his eyes. Understanding washed over him again and again, and it was bitter and salty, and it burned. He knew, finally. He knew, and it felt nothing like he'd thought it would. The puzzle had hollowed him.

Sophie gripped Gordon again, around the arm, and Gordon opened his eyes. Across the room, along the perpendicular wall, was the source of the loud hissing. Three enormous gas furnaces were illuminated weakly by bare bulbs, as if each was being interrogated. A figure moved quickly across the path of light, a moving shadow that Gordon recognized.

Mo was hacking at the base of the nearest furnace with some blunt instrument, pummeling the metal with wide, swinging blows, trying to rip it open like a cooling vein of lava to expose the slow-burning heart. The hissing was the gas pouring out, bleeding like sap. If the smoke wasn't masking it, he was sure the whole place would smell like rotten eggs.

"Sophie, we have to go," Gordon said, but he was surprised and terrified at how calmly he said it, as if muttering in his sleep.

Sophie held him fast as they watched the fire at the heart of the farthest furnace grow before their eyes—it caught the gas as it leaked and puffed up like a beating heart filled to the brim. Mo turned around and ran back toward them quickly. She hopped up on top of the table, and Gordon could hear the creaking, feel the tremor of it. He imagined her, hands on her hips, surveying her work with that hollow and weeping grin.

He coughed heavily. His lungs wracked and scoured. He spat on the floor.

Dianne's head shot down from the top of the table, as if hung upside down. She stared at Gordon with screaming eyes, but her mouth was silent, split in an upside-down grin.

Gordon didn't scream or crawl away. He looked right

back at Mo. Gordon had no fear, only terrible understanding. He saw Dianne there, hidden behind all the pain. And Dianne wasn't a monster. She was a broken mother who'd shattered her psyche to deal with extraordinary loss. Nor was Mo a monster. Mo was the brother that Sophie would never have, the brother that was Dianne's fifth miscarriage. Sophie's twin in the womb. When he never opened his eyes, Dianne took it upon herself to open his eyes for him, to become him. Mo was a personality Dianne created to protect herself and Sophie—the way a big brother ought to.

Mo *had* been watching over Sophie ever since she was born, an imaginary friend that wasn't so imaginary, flitting in and out of Sophie's very real psychosis as often as he flitted in and out from behind her mother's eyes.

And there Mo was, standing above them, trying to protect her still. Gordon had no doubt that Mo was trying to protect Sophie by burning the house down. He didn't know how, but that table, that place, held some sort of talismanic power over Dianne. In all the pictures, it stood safe from the flames.

But pictures were one thing. The reality was that all three of them would die if Gordon couldn't get them out.

Gordon heard a heavy clunk as Mo let the big pipe wrench he'd been swinging fall to the ground in front of them, then he hopped down. Gordon realized that while Mo was perfectly willing to protect Sophie, he didn't care for Gordon at all. In fact, he probably saw Gordon and Dana as trying to part him from Sophie. Most likely, that was why he'd lured Dana almost to her death at the school. Gordon reached for the wrench, but Mo snatched it away, and when Gordon scrabbled toward it, he was baffled by how weakened he was from the smoke. Clumsy. Dizzy. Sleepy.

Mo sidestepped Gordon's grasping hands easily and swung the pipe wrench squarely into his shoulder blade.

The pain was blinding then instantly numbing, but Gordon still could have fought back if he'd wanted to. He saw how weak Dianne was behind Mo's rictus veneer. She was clearly exhausted. She dragged the wrench back to herself slowly, but Gordon couldn't bring himself to hurt her. She'd been hurt so much already. He held his hands out as if to hold her when perhaps he should have lashed out with a kick to bring her low. She scrambled back in a burst, quickly out of reach.

"I'm so sorry," he said. It was all he could say.

Even as he saw her wind up hugely with the wrench again, that time aiming for his head, all he could do was reach for her, as if to hold her hand... and close his eyes.

He waited for the crushing blow. He felt a rustling instead, against his legs, and when he opened his eyes again, he saw Sophie sitting in front of him, between him and Mo. Her legs were clasped to her chest, wrapped by her arms, much the same way he'd first seen her, when she hid beside the hotel bed and he talked her down from her mania as she washed—such a vulnerable child, diminished, yet perhaps the only thing that could give Mo pause.

Mo screamed, a horrible sound, like a newborn animal that finds its mother dead. Gordon was almost relieved when the hissing overtook it... until the furnace exploded.

Mo was thrown forward into Sophie and Sophie thrown backward into Gordon, and all of them were forced back beneath the table, which was swept at the legs down and on top of them, nearly crushing Gordon with its weight as it rolled.

The table saved the three of them from the roiling wave of flame that passed overhead. When Gordon could shrug it aside, he pressed his cheek against the floor and sucked in what he could only assume was the last clean breath of air in the entire house. The furnace was roaring outside of itself, engulfed in a stream of blue fire coming from the valve at its base. The other furnaces were glowing angry red, sagging in the middle. They would ignite soon, he knew. But the effort of moving the table off himself was proving too much. Sophie was pressed against his chest, unmoving. He felt Dianne at his back, also still—all of them in a row. Gordon tried once to move but fell back. The relentless weight of the table began to slowly crush him again.

He realized with shocking clarity and remarkable calmness that they were all going to die there, and none of them deserved it. Certainly not Sophie, but neither Dianne nor him. He might have been too late to save them, but he'd given it everything he had. He'd turned toward the darkness instead of away. His mother would be furious with him for running into the fire, but his mother would understand. And Dana would, too.

He felt a lightening, a freedom. *This must be what dying feels like*. He could finally breathe again, so he took one last breath. Smoke be damned.

CHAPTER THIRTEEN

SIX MONTHS LATER

Dianne West looked at the psychiatrist's chair across from where she sat, waiting patiently. She still hadn't gotten used to her appointments and doubted she ever would. She'd only recently gained the confidence to drive herself to them. She still wore oversized glasses and often a silk scarf, wrapped demurely around her head. The scarf was to cover her short hair—still patchy in many places but growing in better than she had expected—but also to cover her self.

After the fire, all three of them, Dianne, Sophie, and Gordon, had been rushed to the hospital. Sophie was the first to leave, the least injured. She was placed in a private care facility to recuperate, under orders of her father, who legally still had partial custody. Dianne was still in the depths of her disorder at the time she was taken away. Another two weeks passed before she could walk under her own power, another three before she could go an hour without coughing. Then she had to face the aftermath.

That first week, she had her driver roll slowly past the ruins of 8 Long Lane. It was totally destroyed. The burned-out bones of her house jutted here and there like some ancient buried beast slowly exposed by the erosion of time. She told the driver to stop and stepped out. The smell was still strong, the earth still black. That the fire was contained to her lot said less about the ferocity of the blaze than it did about the outrageous size of the Merryville plots. In any other neighborhood in the city, an entire block would have gone up.

No charges were filed—the work of her brother, no doubt. Since the fire, she'd heard that for such a large and consuming blaze, it received little to no attention in the press, either, which she was sure had something to do with Warren as well.

She was a pariah, shunned by her neighbors and whispered after wherever she went in Merryville, so she left. She leased an apartment north of the city in a quiet neighborhood near Druid Lake, where nobody knew her and nobody cared. Then she made the momentous decision to call a psychiatrist.

Only one person would do, but she doubted he would ever be able to see her. She wasn't sure, in fact, if he even had the capacity to see anyone any longer. But she called.

That had been four months before. Today was her twenty-fifth appointment. She heard him coming, clacking down the stairs in his slow way, and she smiled.

GORDON POPE PUSHED OPEN the door to his patient room with his rear and caught it open with the butt end of his cane. He shuffled in and righted himself, smoothing his jacket and coughing lightly into a silk kerchief Dianne had given him on their fourth appointment together—when it became apparent that theirs was, in fact, going to be a long-term professional relationship. He steadied himself. The stars were lessened now, but occasionally they came back. Dianne stood to offer him an arm, but he waved her off.

"I'm fine," he said. "Thank you. Just a bit too much activity."

He walked with three soft clicks to his chair and sat heavily, sighing with contentment as the leather settled around him. Seeing Dianne, an adult, sitting across from him on the small chair built for children still struck him as odd. Then again, she was a small woman, the size of her daughter, easily mistaken for a child from a distance. Nor was Gordon technically going back to adult clients. Dianne was paying the bills, but he was not treating Dianne.

"Are we ready to begin?" Gordon asked.

Dianne nodded.

"Okay, then. I want you to close your eyes and picture yourself under your table again. In your safe space. The only place you feel as if you can be anyone you want to be. It is warm there, and dark, but the stone is pleasantly cool. You rest your head on the stone. You take deep breaths, slowly, and you count back from one hundred..."

Dianne got no further than seventy-eight that time. She was slipping into hypnosis with ease, which was to be expected. The more times she went under, the easier it was to achieve the hypnotic state. They'd worked diligently at that together for a solid month.

"Who am I speaking to?" Gordon asked, his voice calm.

Dianne, eyes still closed, body slack but sitting, replied, "Hi, Dr. Pope. It's Ashley."

Gordon smiled. Ashley was the oldest. As far as Gordon could tell, she was around seventeen. She was the first personality to make herself known to Gordon during their therapy sessions. She considered herself the big sister of the other four and often surfaced when Dianne was incapacitated, either through alcohol or pills. She liked Gordon and recognized Dianne's need for therapy. She knew that the others sometimes ended up hurting Sophie when they were trying to help her.

Ashley was the one who'd drawn the rainbow that brought Gordon downstairs.

That Sophie had never actually drawn any of the pictures was one of the first surprises he learned in treating Dianne's multiple personalities. All of the artwork was done, at various times, by either Ashley, Peter, Sarah, Andrew, or Mo, a pattern that his mother had picked up on after he'd gone rushing to find Simon West.

"Hello, Ashley," Gordon said. "How is it under the table today?"

"It's a bit of a mess. Sarah and Andrew are fighting again. I had to promise them ice cream to shut them up."

"Ice cream usually works," Gordon said.

Dianne ate the ice cream, of course, but it sated the twins. Gordon still had dreams where he came upon their jar. In them, he often had a fear that the contents, their preserved fetuses, would speak to him. They never did, but their silence was more horrible. They were Dianne's third and fourth miscarriages, late enough to cause her great pain. Ashley told him that Dianne had to go downstairs to the cellar, under the table, where she passed both of them on the concrete floor like a frightened animal. Ashley said Dianne wrapped a towel around herself when it was done, jarred them both in memoriam like the first two, and went up to take a shower. She was at a society dinner that night.

Gordon suspected that the passing of the twins was when Dianne's mind cracked, but she'd been trending that way for years. Keeping evidence of a miscarriage wasn't in and of itself unhealthy, but the attachment she'd formed to each was taking her down a dark path. When she became pregnant with twins again, her joy temporarily masked the cracks, but they were there.

Sophie's twin came out first. He never drew a breath. The umbilical cord was wrapped tightly around his tiny neck, and he couldn't be revived. At the time, Dianne thought she'd lost both twins and the horror of Sarah and Andrew was happening all over again. By the time Sophie came, wailing loudly into life, Dianne was already broken even as she wept with joy over her new daughter. The jars started talking to her shortly afterward.

"And how is Peter?" Gordon asked.

"Perfectly quiet," Ashley said.

Gordon had met Peter for the first time the previous week. Peter was shy and rarely came out. He was the one that pranced around the playhouse just before Gordon arrived. He watched Gordon trace his steps around the dust of the playhouse from a special place he knew of on the lawn where nobody could see him, not even the lights. He often slept there, under the trees, for hours and hours and hours, away from everyone. He was a moody fifteen.

Each of Dianne's personalities came out in its own time. Gordon was never sure who would show up. Ashley did most of the time, but sometimes the twins, too. One was never far from the other. They often answered each other's questions. Dianne had a remarkable way of slightly modulating her voice. Andrew spoke faster than Sarah, and Sarah had a minutely higher pitch. Unlike Ashley and Peter, the twins didn't age with time. They stayed the age they would have been on the day that Mo passed. They were frozen in time at four years old.

The only one he had yet to meet again was Mo. Ashley preempted his next question with a surprising answer.

"Mo says he wants to meet you now. For real this time."

Gordon straightened. His goal for months had been to bring Mo out in a safe environment. Since the fire, he'd taken all of his rage and walled off his area of the table. Ashley said it was getting "weird under there." Gordon knew the longer he remained shut away, the greater the chance he would explode forth again, looking to burn.

"Is he sure?" Gordon asked.

"Yeah. But..."

"But what?"

"If I hand off to Mo, I don't know what's gonna happen. Dianne told me to never let him out."

"This is a safe place. Mo can come out here. I have to talk to him if I ever hope to get all of you up on the table."

Up on the table was code for integrating the personalities. Ashley understood it, and so did Dianne, and both were on board, but the twins were scared to leave their nook underneath the table, and Peter liked being alone. Gordon was still working on the three of them but was confident that they would go along with the plan in time.

Mo was a different story.

Ashley let out a big sigh. "Okay," she said. "I'll get him."

Dianne dropped her chin and breathed deeply. All was still. The ticking of the clock was the only sound. Then, very slowly, Dianne's mouth split into a wide grin. She opened her eyes, which was something she'd never done before under hypnosis, and slowly raised her head again until she was staring straight at Gordon.

Gordon remembered the pipe wrench. It took a great deal of personal will to stay rooted to his seat and not shuffle quickly out the door.

"Hello, Mo," Gordon said. His voice wavered a little.

"You took her away from me," Mo whispered, a harsh sound that reminded Gordon unsettlingly of the hiss of the leaking furnaces. He never broke his grin as he spoke, his whisper forced through his teeth.

"Who did I take away?"

"My sister. You took my sister away from me."

"Sophie is safe, Mo. She is sick but getting better every day. Soon, you'll be able to see her again. If you can behave."

Mo gripped the edges of the small chair until his nails bit into the leather. "She needs me," he said. "Nobody else will keep her safe. Who burned the tree house after she fell from it, so that she'd never fall again? Me. Do you think it was Dianne? No. Dianne came to me, frightened and weak, and told me how Sophie was ridiculed at school for her counting and washing, brought to tears in front of everyone in the science labs. Who made sure she'd never get ridiculed at schoolagain?"

"You did," Gordon said.

"I did. I do what nobody else can. And when Sophie gets older and the real horrors of life begin, who do you think will keep her safe then? *Ashley?*" He said his alter personality's name with derision. "She's too busy wrangling the twins. Peter? He's too busy moping around under trees. Dianne can hardly hold her head up with the drinking and pills. So it'll be me. I'll make sure she never gets hurt."

"Dianne is working on the drinking problem, Mo. And the pills. Ashley tells me she doesn't do them anymore."

"Ashley doesn't know everything like she says she does. Peter's started to drink recently."

Gordon took in a slow breath. He'd have to speak with Dianne about that. Wrangling a drinking habit was hard enough when you just had the one personality to deal with. He tried not to let his disappointment show. Integration was a complex process, and they were bound to encounter setbacks, but he knew that most of Dianne's personalities seemed in it for the long haul.

After his outburst, Mo relaxed a bit. His hands eased their grip on the chair, and his smile seemed less manic.

"Why do you smile, Mo?" Gordon asked. "You don't seem happy, but you always smile."

Mo's eyes softened, but his grin hardened.

"I was, once."

"When?"

"When Sophie was born. That was the last time all of us came out at once without fighting or running into each other. Dianne said we were going to lose Sophie. We had prepared for it, prepared to find her under the table, like us. But when she came out and Dianne held her, I was happy she didn't end up under the table with us. I was happy she was forever up top. I was happy then, for a moment."

Gordon took mental note of a powerful insight. Despite Mo's violent words, the only time he'd been happy was when he realized Sophie would live outside of Dianne—would be forever up top.

"You can be up top too, Mo. All of you can be like Sophie if you'll work with Dianne instead of wall yourself off underneath."

Mo was silent, eyes downcast. "I'm going back now," he said after a moment.

"Thanks for talking to me, Mo."

Dianne had already dipped her head. Her smile faded. When she looked up again, Gordon recognized the scared, tired eyes of Dianne herself. She looked exhausted. The sessions took a lot out of her.

"Did we make any progress?" she asked.

"We did," Gordon said. "I'll see you at the same time next week."

AFTER DIANNE WAS GONE, Gordon wrote down all his thoughts from their session. He had a folder for each personality, and most of them were quite substantial, but until then, Mo's had been empty. Gordon finished printing the debrief and slid his first sheet of paper into the folder then sat back. At times, the amount of work he knew was ahead of him with Dianne was overwhelming. But in moments like those, when he could hear the sound of his breakthrough as it settled in the folder, when he could see it with his own eyes, everything was worth it.

He looked at his message machine, an ancient plastic relic from the past, and found it was blinking red. He pressed Play.

"Hello Dr. Pope, this is James Cohn over at Brookhaven Clinic. I'm Sophie's attending physician. You wanted me to call you when the next payments came through, and I can confirm that they have, and I can confirm that they are indeed courtesy of a Mr. Warren Duke. So Sophie is all set. She's progressing nicely although we still think it'll be some time before she's able to check out. As always, you're welcome to follow her notes on our shared system, as her primary care provider. Give us a call with any questions."

Gordon smiled. *So Duke had caved.* Gordon had thought he might. All he'd had to do was figure out why Duke hated him so much. Why they kept crossing paths. And he'd used it to his advantage.

After he was released from the hospital, Gordon went directly to the police department and said he wanted to clear up some miscommunications surrounding the injury of Detective Dana Frisco. He told a slack-jawed member of the arson unit that the Merryville Prep fire was actually intentional. He knew who set it, as did Dana Frisco, who'd risked her life and was injured on the job and would be needing full pay and extended leave to recover.

That got Duke downstairs really quickly.

He took one look at Gordon, taking in his cane and his cough, and the vein at his temple started flickering like purple lightning.

"Would you join me in my office, Dr. Pope," he asked with a forced smile that would have made Mo proud.

Once behind closed doors, he dropped all pretense, and Gordon could see that if the two of them were under other more primitive circumstances, Duke wouldn't have hesitated to kill him—his hate was that strong. And after almost a solid month of grueling rehab, where all Gordon had had to keep him occupied during the pain were his own thoughts, he'd finally figured out why.

Simon West eventually showed him the obvious, what he should have seen all along. When Simon took Sophie under his wing and checked her in to Brookhaven—which even Gordon had to admit was an excellent facility for young children with mental disorders of her magnitude— and he paid for the initial treatments out of his own pocket while Dianne was still in the depths of her psychosis— which was *not* cheap—Gordon ended up marveling at the man. At first, Gordon thought he might have a condition of his own—he'd come off as eccentric and strange—but in the end, he was the sanest of all of them.

That meant that a propensity for mental disorders ran solely through Dianne's line of the family.

The most overlooked aspect of acute psychosis was also

perhaps its most damaging: it ran in the family. Not content to destroy the lives of one or two individuals, it tended to attack entire branches of family trees. And Warren Duke was one of those branches.

"Don't sit down," Duke said, first thing. "You're going to go back down there, say you'd had too much to drink, and walk away before I pick up this phone and end your life forever. Do you understand me, Dr. Pope?"

"I'm not going anywhere, Duke," Gordon said, and he sat down.

Duke sneered at him and started dialing.

"How long have you been hearing voices, Major?"

Duke stopped dialing and slowly hung up the phone.

"Not long, I'd suspect, given how high functioning you are. But they're getting louder, aren't they?"

Duke's silence told Gordon all that he needed to know.

"If it's still early enough, it's easier to treat. But you have to stop fighting against it, projecting your weakness onto your sister and her daughter, and you have to stop taking it out on me."

Duke remained frozen, as if his system was rebooting.

"So here's what's going to happen. You're going to commend Detective Frisco for bravery in the line of duty and grant her full pay while she recovers from her injuries. Then, you're going to commend Detective Marty Cicero for the same, personally. In fact, you owe Marty three times over. When he lifted that table in the basement, he saved your sister, and he saved your niece, and he saved me. And I'm the one continuing to save your sister. That's three favors you owe him. Do you understand me? I'm gonna keep track of them. And last thing: You're paying for the rest of Sophie's treatment, for her life. Do you hear me? And so I know I got through to you,

I want you to make your first payment courtesy of Warren Duke."

Still no movement from Duke, but Gordon thought he'd made his point. He stood to leave. At the door to Duke's office, he paused and turned around. Duke was taking shallow breaths but was otherwise still.

"When you decide you want to take control of your condition, give me a call. I can refer you to some psychiatrists who just might put up with your bullshit long enough to work with you."

He'd left without another word and begun the long process of rehabilitating Dianne West. And sitting there with Mo's file still in hand, a grin on his face, he felt better than he had in a long time. Apparently, he and Warren Duke had finally come to understand one another.

Gordon closed his eyes and leaned back in his chair. His recovery from the fire was a slow process, just like everything in his life those days. The table had torn his ACL and MCL and shredded his meniscus when it hit him, and the doctors said even when fully recovered, he might always walk with a bit of a limp. He was learning to live with it. He just needed a little longer to get places lately, but the good things, the things that mattered, would keep.

Three sharp beeps of a horn woke him from his nap. He checked his phone and found that he'd missed three calls. He checked his watch and cursed. He stood as quickly as he was able, wincing as his knee eased into position underneath him. Then he grabbed his coat and keys and locked the door to his office behind him. Dana's minivan was already at the curb.

"Why don't you *ever* answer your phone, Gordon? We really need to work on this."

"Sorry," he said sheepishly. "I'm taking it off vibrate as soon as I get in the car."

He opened the passenger's side door and found his mother sitting primly in the seat already.

"In the back, dear," she said.

He nodded. "So this is how it is now, huh?"

"Yes, honey. This is how it is."

Gordon pulled open the sliding door with effort but was helped from the inside by Chloe, who opened it the rest of the way.

"Hi, Gord," she said, smiling. "You can sit next to me in the back, 'kay?"

Gordon looked into the far back of the van. It was like spelunking in a cave.

"All the way back?" he asked.

Maria leaned over to him and offered a hand from the captain's chair in the second row. "Here, Dr. Pope, I'll help you up."

Gordon reached for it, and she pulled him up and in. "You don't have to call me Dr. Pope, Maria. You can call me Gordon. Or Gord. Or Gordo. Or anything."

"I like Dr. Pope," she said, smiling.

Several minutes later, Gordon was settled in and buckled up next to Chloe in the far back of the van. He saw Dana's eyes in the rearview mirror. She winked at him.

His mother chimed in from up front. "Now then, all that's settled. Shall we go eat? I know the perfect place."

ABOUT THE AUTHOR

B. B. Griffith writes best-selling fantasy and thriller books. He lives in Denver, CO, where he is often seen sitting on his porch staring off into the distance or wandering to and from local watering holes with his family.

See more at his digital HQ: https://bbgriffith.com

If you like his books, you can sign up for his mailing list here: http://eepurl.com/SObZj. It is an entirely spam-free experience.

ALSO BY B. B. GRIFFITH

The Vanished Series

Follow the Crow (Vanished, #1)

Beyond the Veil (Vanished, #2)

The Coyote Way (Vanished, #3)

Gordon Pope Thrillers

The Sleepwalkers (Gordon Pope, #1)

Mind Games (Gordon Pope, #2)

Shadow Land (Gordon Pope, #3)

The Tournament Series

Blue Fall (The Tournament, #1)

Grey Winter (The Tournament, #2)

Black Spring (The Tournament, #3)

Summer Crush (The Tournament, #4)

Luck Magic Series

Las Vegas Luck Magic (Luck Magic, #1)

Standalone

Witch of the Water: A Novella